情境式

哈啦英文1000句

「圖像導引法」，帶你破冰、不尷聊，自信、舒適、
流暢地用英語閒聊 人生大小事

這一次，用有邏輯的「圖像導引法」來學習流暢地打開英語聊天的話匣子！只要不間斷地閱讀、聽音檔，再大膽地應對、練習口說，你也可以自信地用英語哈啦聊不停！

第 2 章 哈啦滑手機

角色：哈哈（來自台灣）、Lyla（來自美國）

Great ...

How was your weekend?

Yeah ... not bad

Where did you go?

Get your head up! Phubber!

=1=

可愛的情境圖像吸睛，再用小劇場對話破冰，學習更生動。

以趣味的數格漫畫圖像，精準直擊主題情境；再以兩位漫畫主角的對話為借鏡，學習破冰技巧，啟動聊天話題。

1. I am currently work

我現在在大阪的一間旅行社

currently 目前／work fo
based 以……為基地／ O

介紹自己的職業時，可以用以

I work in ＋領域、I work as travel agency based in Osaka.

a company that… 也

company that…

ompanies.「它是一間幫

・關於「介紹職業」，你還能

I work in online education
我做線上教育的。

I'm working as a kinderg
我現在在台北當幼兒園老

a software en

=2=

25 件人生大事＋ 250 個聊天主題＋ 750 個應對擴充句，不尬聊、不句點。

聊天主題明確清楚，讓你從寵物聊到買股、從工作說到父母；橫向→不斷開展話題，縱向→持續深入內容；不怕羞、無冷場、不擔心話題卡住，一來一往，聊天不斷流。

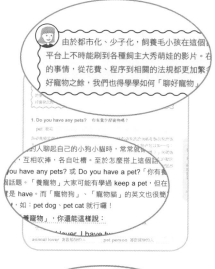

3

關鍵字＋必學詞彙＋慣用語全收錄，英語口說學好學滿

每一話題精準抓出重要關鍵字，快速 catch 聽／說重點；同時補充說明必會或較難單字，即使遇到陌生詞彙也能駕輕就熟！慣用語單元以對話式的設計，能更易理解相關的英語進階使用方式，英文程度更上一層樓。

pick　選擇

set　設立
at stake　有風險
diversify　多樣化
stock market　股市

跟股票有關的慣用語

1. laughing stock　笑柄

哈哈：Look at my hair. It's
　　　stock of the school
　　　看看我的頭髮，
　　　market this sum
Lyla Lyla：Don't worry and the stock market.

3. play with fire　玩火（做冒險的事）
哈哈：I think I'm gonna put in another 10,000 dollars.
　　　我覺得我想再投入 1 萬塊這樣哩？
Lyla：You can't be serious! You're playing with fire!
　　　你在開玩笑吧！你這是在玩火啊！

4. blow it all on　把錢都砸在……上

4

精彩補充大滿貫

◆「你還能這樣說」：更多話題的換個說法及實用文法解析
　EX：Do you have any pets?
　（你有養什麼寵物嗎？）
　換個說法：Do you have a pets?

◆ 異國文化特色、資訊分享
　在學習的過程中，除了分享與主題相關的資訊之外，同時也提醒異地不同文化及生活習慣上的差異，幫助你在與他人互動過程中，不踩雷、不犯忌諱，廣結善緣有好人緣。

◆ 哈啦英文 mp3 音檔
　特聘外師親錄語音檔，250 個聊天主題、750 句擴充例句全都錄。一掃隨聽，時時都能練習道地口語。

由於都市化、少子化，飼養毛小孩在這個
平台上不能刷到各種飼主大秀萌娃的影片。在
的事情，從花費、程序到相關的法規都更加繁
好寵物之餘，我們也得學學如何「聊好寵物」

1. Do you have any pets?　你有養什麼寵物嗎？
　pet　寵物

的人聊起自己的小狗小貓時，常常就會
互相吹捧，各自吐槽。至於怎麼搭上這個話
you have any pets? 或 Do you have a pet?「你有養
話題。「養寵物」大家可能有學過 keep a pet，但在
是 have。而「寵物狗」、「寵物貓」的英文也很簡
，如：pet dog、pet cat 就行囉！

「養寵物」，你還能這樣說：
animal lover　喜歡動物的人　　　pet person　喜歡養寵物的人

🎧 **TRACK 025**

有人出來標榜這是

　　我有很多學生背了很多單字，各種文法規則也能倒背如流，但一開口說英語時，不是結結巴巴，詞不達意，就是一口彆扭的教科書式英語。這些學生，不是他們不夠努力，而是沒有正確用上力。就像一個學游泳的人，拚命地研究流體力學，卻始終不肯下水；一個廚師學徒講得一口好菜，卻連烤箱都不會操作……這種情形很普遍，也很弔詭，即便大家都認同語言學習的終極目的是與人溝通，還是只有為數不多的人在使用正確的方法學習語言。

　　那我們要說「學文法」錯了嗎？

　　其實不然！事實上，在目標語言使用機會匱乏的環境中，通過學習文法規則推導出語言的確效率較高，但問題是：這種「追求效率」的語言學習法能夠幫助我們理解語言，卻無法培養我們的溝通能力，造成這種「知道怎麼用卻不會用」的現象。

　　但生活中難道不是很多事情都是我們「會用卻不知道怎麼用」的嗎？我們的胃每天都在幫我們消化食物，但卻不是所有人都知道胃是怎麼運作的；我們都愛滑手機，但有多少人真的知道觸控面板是怎麼一回事呢？我們天天說著華語，但華語的語法你又了解多少呢？這些例子讓我們思考：我們要朝著「認知」還是「能力」去發力？

　　既然我們的目的是溝通，那我們何不將問題簡單化，直接從溝通層面著手呢？

　　大家想想，平常我們講話時，多半都是以「句子」為單位的吧！但在英文課上，老師一般都要求我們背「單字」、分析「文法」，再將成串的單字根據文法規則組合排列成句子。結構簡單的句子還好，如果是多個子句組成的複雜句，豈不耗上半天時間？

那如果我們將這腦迴路拉直，繞過單字、文法，直接背句子呢？

　　雖然我們不見得理解這個句子的組成邏輯，但我們能夠在溝通時以完整的句子單位作為回應，那不是直接完成溝通任務了嗎？當我們養成背句子的習慣，將句子作為對話的最小單位時，我們可以省掉繁複的思考工序，直接根據語境以句子來回應，雖然這樣不如學習文法有效率、有邏輯，還必須背大量的句子，並反覆練習形成條件反射，但卻是更貼近真實溝通情況，也更相似於母語習得過程的。再者，在具備溝通能力的基礎上去學文法，對語言的認知會更全面，對語言的運用還能達到加乘的效果。

　　這本書根據 25 個話題整理出了 1000 個英文句子，每個句子都是在口語對話中常用的表達法，即使不盡全面也盡量包含了人生中常遇到的各種聊天話題。在這裡我們不談太多的文法，不過度分析語言，我們不只背單字，還直接背句子。只要將這本書慢慢消化吸收後，相信下次和老外聊天時，你會發現你的口語變得更溜了喔！

　　另外，更特別的是：每個章節開始前，我還特別「邀請」了來自台灣的哈哈和來自美國的 Lyla 帶來各種生活小劇場，來自截然不同文化的兩人，在語言和想法上會碰撞出什麼令人噴飯笑話呢？就讓我們一起來看看吧！

CONTENTS
目錄

全書音檔連結

因各家手機系統不同，若無法直接掃描，仍可以至
（https://tinyurl.com/3dvcajya）
電腦結雲端下載！

第１章 哈啦寵物

角色：哈哈（來自台灣）、Lyla（來自美國）

由於都市化、少子化，飼養毛小孩在這個世代已成了一個超夯的流行，社群平台上不時能刷到各種飼主大秀萌娃的影片。在國外，養寵物更是一個為人重視的事情，從花費、程序到相關的法規都更加繁多、先進。因此，在國外，除了養好寵物之餘，我們也得學學如何「聊好寵物」喔！

1. Do you have any pets?　你有養什麼寵物嗎？

> pet　寵物

兩個養寵物的人聊起自己的小狗小貓時，常常就像兩個家庭的爸媽在聊自家的孩子一樣，互相吹捧，各自吐槽。至於怎麼搭上這個話題呢？我們可以問一句：Do you have any pets? 或 Do you have a pet?「你有養什麼寵物嗎？」來開啟這個話題。「養寵物」大家可能有學過 keep a pet，但在口語上更常搭配的動詞其實是 have。而「寵物狗」、「寵物貓」的英文也很簡單，只要在名詞前面加上 pet，如：pet dog、pet cat 就行囉！

- 關於「養寵物」，你還能這樣說：

I'm a big animal lover. I have two dogs and a cat.
我超喜歡動物的，我養兩隻狗和一隻貓。

No. I'm not a pet person.
沒有，我不太喜歡寵物。

I don't like large pets, but I'm fine with smaller animals.
我不喜歡大型寵物，但小動物我還 ok。

animal lover　喜歡動物的人	pet person　喜歡寵物的人

2. My landlord doesn't allow pets. 我的房東不讓養寵物。

> landlord 房東／ allow 允許

和外國人聊天時經常出現尷尬、斷流的情況，通常不是因為沒話聊，而是不知道怎麼表達。好比接續第一個話題的 Do you have a pet?「你有養什麼寵物嗎？」如果只回答了一個 No!「沒有」很容易就把話題推入一個尷尬的句點，甚至會讓對方覺得你有點難聊呢！如果我們能在 No! 之後補充「不能養寵物」的原因，就能讓對話繼續流動起來，避免一字回答。

- 關於「不能養寵物」，你還能這樣說：

  I'm allergic to animals.
  我對動物過敏。

  I can't afford a pet.
  我養不起寵物。

  I'm too busy to own a pet.
  我太忙了沒時間養寵物。

allergic 過敏的	**afford** 付得起	**own** 擁有

3. What breed is it? 牠是什麼品種的？

> breed 品種

就像在美國，走在路上散步時向路過的陌生人微笑打招呼是個基本禮儀一樣，帶著小傢伙出門遛遛，也要準備幾句向「同行人」交流的英文句子，因為大部分的寵物主人都會很熱情地過來跟你聊聊你家的小寵物喔！比如：You've got a cute dog.「你的狗好可愛。」、Oh my gosh! She's adorable!「哇！她好可愛！」、Is this your dog?「這是你的狗嗎？」、What type of dog is it?「牠是什麼狗？」

- 關於「寵物 Q & A」，你還能這樣說：

  How old is he?
  他幾歲了？

What's his name?
他叫什麼名字？

My dog is actually a she.
我的狗其實是個女孩。

actually 其實

4. Can I stroke him?　我可以摸他嗎？

stroke 撫摸

看到 Q 萌的毛小孩，誰不會想要摸一把咧！？這裡的「摸寵物」一般不會用大家通常會第一個想到的 touch，而是 pet 或 stroke，因此，pet a dog 或 stroke a dog 就是「撫摸小狗」。

• 關於「摸寵物」，你還能這樣說：

Will he bite me?
他會咬我嗎？

Her fur is so soft.
她的毛好柔軟。

He likes to be scratched under the chin.
他喜歡別人騷他下巴。

bite 咬	fur 毛皮	scratch 騷
chin 下巴		

5. It's learned quite a few tricks.　牠已經學會好幾個技能了。

quite a few 好幾個 ／ trick 技能

小貓、小狗的「技能」在英文中一般會說 trick。因此，我們在聊小寵物的十八般武藝時，就可以問：Does she know any tricks? 或 Can he do any tricks?「她／他會什麼技能？」回答時，可以說：She's learned quite a few tricks.「她已經學會好幾個技能了。」

- 關於「寵物技能」，你還能這樣說：

Play dead.
裝死。

Roll over.
翻滾。

Spin.
轉圈。

play 演	roll 打滾	spin 旋轉

6. She's hypersensitive to sound.　她對聲音特別敏感。

hypersensitive 過於敏感的 / sound 聲響

每隻寵物都像主人的親生小孩一樣，和別人聊起時特別會散發出慈父慈母的光輝，尤其是聊到寵物的個性時，真的會有種搬出育兒經、媽媽經的感覺呢！以下幾句提供給各位寵物爸爸媽媽們，學會用英文哈啦寵物的個性。

- 關於「寵物個性」，你還能這樣說：

It gets excited a lot.
牠經常激動。

He's much more submissive than before.
他比起以前順從多了。

He gets skittish around strangers.
他在陌生人面前會比較膽小。

excited 興奮的	submissive 順從的	skittish 膽小的
stranger 陌生人		

7. I'm more of a dog person. 我更喜歡狗。

> more of... 更偏向

養貓好還是養狗好？這個百年辯題似乎始終沒有一個主流的定論。貓貓狗狗各有所好，有人說：小狗是過動兒，熱情如火；小貓是自閉兒，高冷孤僻。這兩個截然不同的性格各自吸引了大批的粉絲。如果要說「更喜歡……」，我們可以用 more of a...person 來表達，如：I'm more of a dog person.「我更喜歡狗。」

• 關於「貓狗比一比」，你還能這樣說：

Dogs are more loyal than cats.
狗比貓更忠誠。

Dogs are too needy.
狗太黏人了。

Cats are easier to train than dogs.
貓比狗更好訓練。

loyal 忠誠的	needy 黏人的	train 訓練

8. What symptoms did you notice? 牠有什麼症狀？

> symptom 症狀 / notice 注意到

隨著動物醫學的發展，現在的寵物在醫療上幾乎都可以享有和人類一般的待遇了。因此，在帶自己的寵物去看病時，如何和寵物醫生對話也成了一個重要的技能了。一般的獸醫在問診時，通常會問到：What symptoms did you notice? 或 What seems to be the problems?「牠有什麼症狀？」幾個很好描述寵物健康問題的句型有：It has difficulty V-ing.「牠……有困難。」、It seems to struggle to Vr.「牠似乎……很吃力。」、It has a ＋症狀 .「牠有……症狀。」。

• 關於「寵物生病」，你還能這樣說：

I think he has a fever.
他好像發燒了。

He's been vomiting.
他一直嘔吐。

He's lost his appetite.
他沒什麼胃口。

fever 發燒	vomit 嘔吐	appetite 食慾

9. I want to take my dog to a vet for some vaccinations.
我想帶我的狗去給獸醫打疫苗。

vet 獸醫／vaccination 疫苗

學完了帶寵物看病，我們接著來學學「寵物的保養和登記」，包含：vaccination「打疫苗」、get it vaccinated「打疫苗」、microchip「植晶片」、neuter「結紮」和 trim「剪毛」等。其中，vaccination 是指「打疫苗」的動作，而「疫苗」本身的英文是 vaccine。

- 關於「寵物保養」，你還能這樣說：

I'm planning to get my dog microchipped.
我計畫要帶我的狗去植晶片。

I'm thinking about neutering my dog.
我在考慮帶我的狗去結紮。

I trim its coat every two months.
我每兩個月幫牠剪一次毛。

microchip 植晶片	neuter 結紮	trim 修剪
coat 毛皮		

10. I have a friend who has a snake.　我有一個朋友養蛇。

> snake　蛇

除了小狗、小貓外，相信很多人會養或聽說朋友有養一些相對冷門的寵物，像是：蛇、蠍子、松鼠、蜥蜴之類的。最後，我們就來學學哈啦奇葩寵物的英文句子吧！

• 關於「各種寵物」，你還能這樣說：

My friend even has an instagram account for her rabbit. It's got a lot of followers.
我朋友還有一個 IG 帳號專門給她的兔子，關注的人超多的。

Looking at my fish really helps me to relieve stress.
盯著我的魚可以幫我解壓。

I have never heard of anybody having a pet spider before.
我以前從來沒聽說過有人養蜘蛛當寵物的。

account 帳號	follower 追蹤者	relieve 解放
stress 壓力	hear of 聽說	spider 蜘蛛

 跟寵物有關的慣用語

1. pet peeve　個人覺得討厭的事物

哈哈：I really can't stand their poor service.
　　　我真受不了他們那麼差勁的服務。

Lyla：Neither can I. It's my biggest pet peeve.
　　　我也是，我對差勁的服務也很受不了。

2. teacher's pet 　老師的寵兒

哈哈：It's amazing that your primary school teacher still remembers
　　　you.
　　　妳的小學老師竟然還記得妳，真是神奇。

Lyla：Of course! I was always my teacher's pet before.
　　　那當然啦！我以前可是老師的寵兒呢！

3. dog-gone 　超級

哈哈：How was the movie last night?
　　　昨天晚上的電影怎麼樣？

Lyla：It was dog-gone good.
　　　超讚的！

4. cat got my tongue 　說不出話

哈哈：Why didn't you say you like her too?
　　　為什麼妳不說妳也喜歡他呢？

Lyla：I don't know. I was like cat got my tongue.
　　　不知道啊！我就是一時說不出話。

5. You can't teach an old dog new tricks. 　老狗學不了新把戲。

哈哈：I gave up. They still won't listen to my advice.
　　　我放棄了，他們還是不聽我的建議。

Lyla：Deal with it! You can't teach an old dog new tricks.
　　　習慣就好，老狗學不了新把戲。

第 2 章　哈啦滑手機

角色：哈哈（來自台灣）、Lyla（來自美國）

滑手機大概已經超越吸菸成為現代人最難戒除的習慣了吧！不管何時何地都能滑，不僅能站著滑、坐著滑、蹲著滑，還能躺著滑，不時還會滑到手機砸臉，不滑個幾下就會手癢難耐。無奈手機的誘惑力實在太大了，不當個 phubber 就會有 FOMO。這些詞又是什麼意思呢？身為內行的低頭族，讓我們繼續看下去！

1. I really need to get my hands on an iPhone now.
我想買 iPhone 了。

> get one's hands on 入手

現在各大廠牌的手機通常都是一年一新機，每次廣告都看得讓人心頭癢癢，忍不住想入手一台。而「入手」的英文，我們一般都會直覺地想到 buy，但這邊我們也學一個新片語：get one's hands on「把手放到……上」，也就是「取得」的意思。至於「手機」的英文詞彙也有很多種，如：cell phone、mobile phone、cell 等，但其實最常用的還是最簡單的 phone 這個字。

• 關於「換手機」，你還能這樣說：

I'm about to retire my phone.
我要讓我這支手機退休了。

I'm confused between iOS and Android.
我不知道要買蘋果的還是安卓的。

I'm a real Apple fan. I've never owned a non-Apple smartphone.
我是個超級果粉。我從來沒有用過不是蘋果的手機。

be about to 即將要	retire 使退役	confused 感到困惑的
own 擁有	smartphone 智慧型手機	

2. I'm looking for something in the mid-range.
我在找中等價位的機型。

> mid-range 中等範圍

大家有過在國外把手機弄丟而被迫要買新手機時的窘境嗎？這時如果英文又不通，沒辦法順利地買到自己需要的手機，那簡直令人崩潰！買手機時，最重要的就是價位和配置需求了。首先，「價位」的英文我們會用 range 這個字。「中等價位」便是 mid-range；「中高價位」是 upper mid-range；「中低價位」lower mid-range；而「低價」、「陽春」、「入門款」我們可以說 basic 或 entry-level。至於「配置」，我們可以用這個句型：I am looking for something with...「我在找有……的機型。」

• 關於「物色手機」，你還能這樣說：

I'm aiming for a cheap, basic phone just for making phone calls and texts.
我在找單純可以打電話、傳簡訊的便宜陽春手機。

I'd like to spend maybe four, five hundred maximum.
我的預算上限大概是四、五百元。

I'm looking for the best camera for photography.
我想找最好的拍照手機。

aim for 尋找	basic 基礎的	text 簡訊
maximum 上限	photography 攝影	

3. Does it have a facial recognition login? 它有臉部辨識功能嗎？

facial 臉部的／ recognition 辨識／ login 登入

近年來智慧型手機的配置越來越五花八門，不是科技宅還真不知道怎麼把所有標榜的功能都用上呢！以下列舉幾個較常接觸的功能和配置。而當要詢問手機是否搭載某某功能時，我們可以問：Does it have...?「它有……功能嗎？」

[註]：智慧型手機常用功能：face unlock 臉部解鎖／ fingerprint scanner 指紋辨識／ wireless charging 無線充電／ fast charging 快速充電／ dual SIM card support 雙 SIM 卡／ virtual assistant 虛擬助手／ water resistance 防水／ front camera 前鏡頭／ rear camera 後鏡頭／ ultra-wide camera 超廣角鏡頭

- 關於「手機配置」，你還能這樣說：

How much storage space do you have on your phone?

你的手機容量有多大？

Where's its headphone jack?

它的耳機孔在哪？

It is equipped with dual cameras.

它裝有雙鏡頭。

storage 儲存	space 空間	headphone 耳機
jack 孔	be equipped with 裝有	dual camera 雙鏡頭

4. You can hold down the homescreen button and the volume down key to take a screenshot.

你可以同時長按主屏幕鍵和減音量來照螢幕快照。

hold down 按下／ homescreen button 主屏幕鍵／ volume down key 減音量鍵／ screenshot 螢幕快照

關於各種手機功能的操作問題，我們可以問：How do I...? 比如：How do I take a screenshot?「螢幕快照怎麼拍？」、How do I use Siri?「Siri 怎麼用？」、How do I download apps?「應用程式怎麼下載？」等。特別注意：很多人會說成 How to...? 但即使在口語英語中，這也是文法錯誤的句子喔！

- 關於「手機操作（一）」，你還能這樣說：

Press the homescreen button to launch Siri.

按下主屏幕鍵來啟動 Siri。

Tap the clock icon to set an alarm clock.

點擊時鐘圖示來設置鬧鐘。

Swipe up from the bottom edge to close the app.

從螢幕底端上滑來關閉應用程式。

press 按壓	launch 啟動	tap 點擊
icon 圖示	set 設置	alarm clock 鬧鐘
swipe 滑	bottom edge 底端	app 應用程式

5. You need to punch in the PIN number to unlock it.

你需要輸入密碼才能解鎖它。

> punch in 輸入／PIN（personal identification number）密碼／
> unlock 解鎖

punch 原本是「用拳頭打擊」的意思，在本句的 punch in 中則是表示「按按鍵輸入」，例如：在提款機「輸入密碼」便是 punch in the password。而在手機上「輸入密碼」也可以說 punch in the PIN number。基本上，PIN 和 password 性質是一樣的，但 PIN 通常只包含數字，而 password 則可包含數字、字母、符號等。

• 關於「手機操作（二）」，你還能這樣說：

Please switch your phone to vibrate mode.
請將你的手機調成震動模式。

Sorry, I didn't hear the phone ring. I had it set to silent.
抱歉，我沒聽到手機響。我把它調成靜音了。

Press and hold the power button to hard reboot the phone.
長按電源鍵來強制重啟手機。

switch 轉換	vibrate 震動	mode 模式
ring 鈴響	silent 靜音	hard reboot 強制重啟

6. Do you have an iPhone charger? 你有 iPhone 的充電線嗎？

> charger 充電線

現代人使用手機的頻率非常高，因此，手機電池便成了我們第二生命般的存在。出門在外時，通常也會隨身帶一顆 power bank，也就是「行動電源」。但當不幸手邊沒有行充時，我們就需要向別人借充電線，英文可以這樣說：

Do you have an iPhone charger?「你有 iPhone 的充電線嗎？」如果是要指「傳輸線」，不是用 line 喔！而是 cable。

• 關於「手機電池」，你還能這樣說：

My battery is dying. My phone's about to power down.
我的電池快沒電了，我的手機快關機了。

My phone can last all day on a single charge.
我的手機充一次電就可以撐一整天。

My phone battery won't charge. Weird.
我的手機電池充不進電，好奇怪。

battery 電池	dying 快死的	power down 關機
last 持續	single 單次	charge 充電
weird 奇怪的		

7. Do you have an unlimited data plan?　你有網路吃到飽嗎？

unlimited 無限的／ data plan 網路方案

手機的「網路方案」英文叫 data plan。「吃到飽」叫 unlimited，而限定流量的方案我們可以説：I have ＋數字＋ gigabytes of data per month.「我用一個月……GB 的流量。」如果自己的流量用完了，需要向別人借流量，可以説：Can you turn on your personal hotspot for me?「你可以開熱點給我用一下嗎？」而「連上熱點」我們可以説 join the hotspot 或 connect to the hotspot。

• 關於「手機網路」，你還能這樣說：

I normally use a prepaid SIM card.
我一般都用預付卡。

I have 10 gigabytes of data per month.
我一個月有 10GB 的流量。

I've used up my data.
我的流量用完了。

8. I left my phone in a taxi. 我把手機丟在計程車上了。

> leave 遺留／ phone 手機

現在的手機幾乎承載了我們所有的個資，包含私人的照片、影片甚至是信用卡資訊，一旦弄丟或被扒走真的是件令人頭疼的事。雖然現在有很多方式可以定位到我們遺失的手機，但剛發現手機弄丟時，通常還是會先四周找找問問，這時候我們就可以說：I left my phone in the...「我把手機丟在……了。」或 I lost my phone. Can you help me track it?「我的手機丟了，你可以幫我找一下嗎？」

• 關於「手機不見」，你還能這樣說：

Where's my phone?
我的手機呢？

Have you seen my phone?
你有看到我的手機嗎？

Can you ring my phone for me?
你可以打一下我的手機嗎？

> ring 打電話

9. I can't hear you. The reception is bad. 我聽不見你，收訊很差。

> reception 收訊

當手機收訊不好或「不想跟對方繼續聊」時（誤），我們便可以說：The reception is bad. I can't hear you.「收訊很差，我聽不見你。」其他的說法還有：The reception is choppy.「收訊斷斷續續的。」、You're breaking up a little.「你有點斷斷續續的。」、I lost service.「我沒有收訊了。」

• 關於「手機問題」，你還能這樣說：

It's running so slow after the update.
它升級之後跑得好慢。

My phone is starting to show its age. It's so glitchy.

我的手機開始老化了，好卡。

The touch screen is not as responsive as usual.

這觸屏不像以前那麼靈敏了。

| update 升級 | glitch 多故障的 | touch screen 觸屏 |
| responsive 反應快的 | | |

10. You're phubbing me.　你一直在滑手機，都不理我。

> phub 埋頭滑手機

手機毫無疑問地為我們帶來了巨大的便利，但同時也造成了一定程度的人際疏離。因此，2015 年的五月便誕生了這個新單字 phubbing。這個字是由 phone「電話」和 snub「冷落」兩個字結合而成的，故名思義就是「一直滑手機而冷落某人」的意思，而這種人我們就叫做 phubber。下次，如果你的家人朋友對你施以科技冷漠時，你便能跟他（她）說：Stop phubbing me!「別再滑手機了！」

- 關於「低頭族」，你還能這樣說：

Don't be such a phubber.

別再當低頭族了。

Get your head out of your phone.

別在看手機了。

You're too addicted to your phone.

你手機成癮太嚴重了。

| phubber 低頭族 | be addicted to 對……上癮的 |

1. FOMO（Fear of Missing Out） 資訊錯失恐慌症；邊緣恐懼症

哈哈：I don't know why, but I just can't help checking my Facebook every once in a while.

不知道為什麼，我時不時就想看一下我的臉書。

Lyla：You have FOMO, dude.

你得了邊緣恐懼症了。

2. My battery is low. 我手機快沒電了。（掛電話藉口）

哈哈：You know what! I had the weirdest dream last night. I dreamed of a bear...

你知道嗎！我昨天晚上做了一個好奇怪的夢，我夢到一隻熊……

Lyla：Sorry, my battery is low. I gotta go.

不好意思，我手機快沒電了，我先掛了。

3. play phone tag 互打電話但都接不到的情況

哈哈：Have you got hold of your sister?

妳聯絡上妳姊了嗎？

Lyla：No. We've been playing phone tag today.

還沒，我們今天一直互相打來打去都沒接到。

4. smartphone zombie 低頭族

哈哈：Hold on a sec. I need to finish sending this message first.

等等，我要先傳完這封訊息。

Lyla：Come on! Get your head up! You smartphone zombie.

拜託！把頭抬起來好嗎！你這個低頭族！

5. give me a buzz 打電話給我

哈哈：I gotta go. My mom's waiting for me.

我得走了，我媽在等我呢！

Lyla：OK. Give me a buzz when you get home.

好，到家打給我。

第３章 哈啦科技

角色：哈哈（來自台灣）、Lyla（來自美國）

活在電子時代，科技充斥著我們的生活，電腦、手機、網路及各種高端科技產品，往往讓人覺得好像必須用很艱澀、高深的詞彙才能表達，但其實你不用當個科技宅、電子通，也能用一些簡單的詞彙侃侃聊科技喔！很多時候，英文說得不夠道地，只是我們不知道如何把我們已經會的詞彙正確地拼裝在一起而已。以下，就讓我們來一起哈啦科技學英文吧！

1. I'm not a tech-savvy person.　我對科技產品不太了解。

> tech-savvy　精通科技的

我們常說的「3C 通」、「科技宅」，在英文中，我們通常會用：tech-savvy、computer geek、computer nerd、computer expert 等名詞來表達。另外，也可以用形容詞的 geeky 和 nerdy 來稱呼「電腦阿宅」或非常精通電腦的達人。

• 關於「科技達人」，你還能這樣說：

Terry is a total computer geek.
Terry 是個電腦宅。

Dustin is a big computer nerd.
Dustin 是個電腦宅。

Are you a computer expert?
你很懂電腦嗎？

geek 怪胎	nerd 書呆子	expert 專家

2. I'm looking to replace my old laptop.　我在想要換電腦。

> look to...　想要……／ replace　代替／ laptop　筆電

中文裡的「買新電腦」，我們常會說「換電腦」，因此，一個常見的中式英文句子便是：I'm going to change my computer. 但正確的英文應該是：I'm going to get a new computer.、I'm going to buy a new computer. 或是 I'm going to replace my computer.。另外，也可以用 be looking to... 「想要……」，如：I'm looking to get a new computer.

- 關於「買新電腦」，你還能這樣說：

I really need to get a computer that's more up-to-date.
我真的需要買一台比較新型的電腦。

It's time for me to get a new laptop.
我該換電腦了。

I need to upgrade my computer.
我需要升級我的電腦了。

up-to-date 最近的	upgrade 升級

3. If you have a good budget, I would suggest you go for an iPhone.
如果你預算夠的話，我會建議你買 iPhone。

budget 預算／ suggest 建議／ go for 選擇

蘋果系統和微軟系統到底誰好誰壞，這個世紀辯題一直懸而未決！當我們在討論買什麼系統的電腦或科技產品時，非常有可能需要加入這個戰局的喔！因此，這邊的幾個句型就能派上用場了！其中，一個非常常見的「如果要我選的話…」，我們可以說：If I were to choose, ... 或 If I had to choose, ...。這兩句的動詞用過去式是因為使用了與現在事實相反的假設語氣來表達委婉的語氣。話說回來，不管這場辯論誰勝誰負，我相信過程中一定會聽到：Once a Mac user, always a Mac user.「一朝果粉，終身果粉。」這個經典名句吧！

- 關於「選擇科技產品」，你還能這樣說：

If I had to choose, I would probably go for a Mac.
如果我要選的話，我可能會選 Mac。

I'm a die-hard Android user.
我是個死忠的安卓用戶。

I switched over to a Mac a year ago.
我一年前開始改用 Mac。

| probably 可能 | die-hard 死忠的 | user 用戶 |
| switch 改變 | | |

4. Its latest camera technology can stack up against other bigger brands. 它的最新拍照技術可以和其他大廠牌的匹敵。

latest 最新的／ technology 技術／ stack up against 與……匹敵／ brand 品牌

在日常對話中，我們不需要很專業、很準確的詞彙也能順利地談論相關話題。比如：關於「拍照技術」，我們不需要談到解析度、像素、畫幅等字眼，只要說 camera technology，對方就一定能聽懂了。即使是母語人士，也不見得知道那麼多專業術語的，反而，當他們聽到過於生僻的詞彙時，還需要一點時間反應呢！

• 關於「科技產品的優點」，你還能這樣說：

It has the state-of-the-art fingerprint recognition technology.
它搭載了最先進的指紋辨識技術。

It has all the bells and whistles.
它擁有各種炫酷的功能。

It features the most cutting-edge technology.
它搭載了最新潮的技術。

| state-of-the-art 最先進的 | fingerprint 指紋 | recognition 識別 |
| bells and whistles 炫酷的功能 | feature 搭載 | cutting-edge 尖端的 |

5. The biggest selling point of this laptop is its long battery life.

這台筆電最大的賣點就是它的電池壽命很長。

> selling point 賣點／ battery 電池

買電腦和各種 3C 產品時，常常就是透過 word of mouth「口耳相傳」來互相推薦的。因此，我們也需要學學如何用英文來描述自己的電腦介面或功能。

• 關於「科技產品的特色」，你還能這樣說：

My favorite part is its intuitive interface.
我最喜歡的就是它非常直覺性的介面。

This app is notorious for hogging disk space.
這個應用程式非常佔磁碟空間。

It's pretty user-friendly.
它用起來非常順手。

intuitive 直覺的	interface 介面	app 應用程式
notorious 惡名昭彰的	hog 佔據	disk 磁碟
user-friendly 操作便捷的		

6. It does not come with SD card slots. 它沒有記憶卡插槽。

> come with 具有／ SD card 記憶卡／ slot 插槽

談論電腦有什麼裝置或功能時，除了 have 之外，我們還可以用 come with...「配有……」、feature「以……為特點」、come in...「有……種類」等，適時地變換動詞的使用來增添詞彙的豐富性，也能讓口語聽起來更自然。

• 關於「科技產品配置」，你還能這樣說：

It comes in four colors.
它有四種顏色。

It works well for video calls.
它的視訊通話功能滿好的。

This one has the latest Intel processor.

這台有最新的 Intel 處理器。

come in　有	video call　視訊通話	processor　處理器

7. The hidden files have been eating up your disk space.

這些隱藏檔案一直吃掉你的硬碟空間。

> hidden　隱藏的／file　檔案

用英文描述電腦的問題也是一個很重要的技能。我們不用學很艱深的術語，只需要善用一些形象化的動詞就能有效地傳達意思。其中，eat up 是一個非常形象的動詞片語，意思是「佔據」。比如：The files are eating up your disk space. 「這些檔案正在佔據你的磁碟空間。」

• 關於「科技產品的問題」，你還能這樣說：

Your memory is maxed out.

你的記憶體滿爆了。

It slows everything down to a crawl.

它讓整個系統都跑得超慢。

My old laptop is just wheezing and slow.

我的舊筆電一直嗡嗡叫，還跑得很慢。

memory　記憶體	max out　滿爆	crawl　爬
wheeze　嗡嗡叫		

8. My computer died.　我的電腦壞了。

> die　死掉

「擬人化」也是口語英語中很常用到的修辭法。比如：My computer died. 「我的電腦壞了。」、It doesn't want to shut down. 「它不想關機。」、I had a few hiccups with my computer. 「我的電腦出了點問題。」聽到別人的電腦壞了，我

們可以問：Have you backed up your computer?「你有把資料備份起來嗎？」
或 Did you take it to the computer shop?「你的電腦送修了嗎？」

- 關於「科技產品壞掉」，你還能這樣說：

Do you know what's wrong with my computer?

你知道我的電腦怎麼了嗎？

I think my computer's got a virus.

我覺得我的電腦中毒了。

Is there any way to fix it?

有辦法修理嗎？

virus 病毒	fix 修理

9. Why don't you go live in a cave?　你為什麼不回山洞住？

> cave 山洞

曾經因為搞不定科技產品被笑嗎？現在換你來學幾句嘲笑別人科技白痴的英文句子，以備不時之需吧！

- 關於「科技白痴」，你還能這樣說：

I can't blame you for not knowing this. You caveman.

你不知道我也不能怪你，你這山頂洞人。

This is over my head.

我對這個一竅不通。

There's no way I can figure it out.

我永遠都不可能搞懂這個。

blame 責備	caveman 原始人	figure out 理解

10. We must find a way to keep up with the technology advancement or we'll get left behind.

我們要想辦法跟上科技發展的腳步，否則我們會被落下的。

> keep up with 跟上／ advancement 發展／ left behind 落後的

Technology. Can't live with it. Can't live without it.「科技這種東西，不敢太相信，但沒有也不行。」人類發展科技似乎已經到了一個不可逆的、越發越張狂的程度。當一切的看似不可能都即將變成現實時，你是迫不及待還是心生畏懼呢？最後，我們來學學如何用英文感嘆科技發展的光速吧！

- 關於「科技發展」，你還能這樣說：

Technology changes so fast year after year.
科技一年一年地更迭好迅速。

We can't keep up with how fast technology is evolving.
我們趕不上科技的變遷。

Technology is moving faster than ever before.
科技的發展前所未見地快速。

> evolve 演化

 跟科技有關的慣用語

1. reinvent the wheel 多此一舉

哈哈：After shooting, we still need to edit it, which is gonna take ages.
拍完片之後，我們還要編輯，到時候一定很耗時。

Lyla：We don't need to reinvent the wheel. We could just hire someone to do it.
不需要多此一舉吧！我們可以直接雇人來編輯。

2. light years ahead　遙遙領先

哈哈：How's your project going so far? I'm already collecting data.

　　　妳的專案進行的怎麼樣了？我已經在蒐集數據囉！

Lyla：Haha! Light years ahead of you. I'm finalizing it already.

　　　哈哈！遙遙領先你呢！我已經在收尾了！

3. well-oiled machine　運行順利

哈哈：How's everything with your team?

　　　妳們的團隊最近如何？

Lyla：Pretty good. We had a new team leader. It's now running like a well-oiled machine.

　　　滿好的。我們來了一位新組長。現在整個團隊運行的非常順利。

4. bells and whistles　華而不實的東西

哈哈：How's your new phone so far?

　　　妳的手機還好用嗎？

Lyla：It's okay. It came with all the bells and whistles, but I don't really know how to use them.

　　　還可以囉！它有很多酷炫的功能，但我還真的不太會用。

5. cog in the machine　重要的一份子

哈哈：I don't think people appreciate my work at all.

　　　我覺得大家都看不到我的付出。

Lyla：Don't say that. You're an important cog in the machine.

　　　別這麼說，你是很重要的一份子。

第 4 章　哈啦網路

角色：哈哈（來自台灣）、Lyla（來自美國）

過去，人類從農村往城市遷徙，現在，人類則是集體從現實世界搬往網路世界。在這劇烈的變動中，我們的語言變得更加豐富，許多網路世界的新詞彙也成為了人們口中的流行語。你知道「網紅」、「爆紅」、「加好友」和「刪好友」的英文怎麼說嗎？一起來緊跟流行，哈啦網路吧！

1. Look it up on Google. 上谷歌查一下。

Google 谷歌

各種強大的搜尋引擎，讓人們獲取資訊於彈指之間，但同時也讓許多人遇到問題時懶得動腦，或根本不想幫忙，而是直接來一句：Look it up on Google.「上谷歌查一下。」或是直接拿 Google 當動詞，如：Google it!「去 Google 查！」唉！在擔心人類和人工智慧發生戰爭前，我們自己可能需要先煩惱怎樣別讓人類的智商退化地太快吧！

• 關於「查資料」，你還能這樣說：

Google it.
上谷歌查一下。

Let me Google that for you.
我幫你 Google 一下。

I'd probably recommend you do a Google search.
我可能會建議你上 Google 去搜尋一下。

probably 可能	recommend 建議	search 搜尋

2. I ordered it on Amazon. 我在亞馬遜上訂的。

order 訂購／ Amazon 亞馬遜

隨著網購的普及和便利，以前人們問 Where did you get it?「你在哪買的？」時，我們可能會說 I bought it from the new Nike store.「我在那間新開的 Nike 店買的。」而現在可能更多地會說 I ordered it on Amazon.「我在亞馬遜上訂的。」或 I bought it on Taobao.「我在淘寶上買的。」

- 關於「網購」，你還能這樣說：

You got another package today.
你今天又有新包裹了。

The shipping is taking forever.
送貨比龜速還慢。

I got crazy discounts on them.
我用超低特價買到那些東西。

| package 包裹 | shipping 發貨 | discount 折扣 |

3. I'm streaming it on my phone.　我直接在手機上看。

> stream 串流

stream 的意思是「線上串流播放」，也就是不需事先下載，而直接在網路上即時觀賞或收聽，也可以翻譯成「刷」。因此，「刷那部影集」我們可以說：stream that series。而「影音串流平台」我們可以說 streaming site，「影音串流軟體」則是 streaming app。

- 關於「網路電影」，你還能這樣說：

I'm watching a new online series on Netflix.
我在 Netflix 上看一部新出的網路影集。

Do you have to sign up?
你需要註冊嗎？

Where can I download it?
我可以在哪裡下載？

| series 影集 | sign up 註冊 | download 下載 |

4. Add me on Facebook. I'll totally confirm.　加我臉書，我一定同意。

add 添加／ Facebook 臉書／ totally 一定／ confirm 確認

我們中文說「加我臉書」的「加」就是用 add，而整句則是 add me on Facebook，記住不是 add my Facebook 喔！同樣地，「加我 Line」不是 add my Line，而是 add me on Line，其他聊天軟體也可以此類推。此外，「加好友」我們還可以說：friend me，此處的 friend 作動詞用，相反地，「刪好友」則是 unfriend me。

• 關於「社群媒體」，你還能這樣說：

I'm gonna block him.
我要封鎖他。

I am unfriended.
我被刪好友了。

She hasn't accepted my friend request.
她還沒接受我的加好友邀請。

block 封鎖	unfriend 刪除好友	accept 接受
request 要求		

5. Did you see what he tweeted yesterday?
你有看到他昨天發的推特嗎？

tweet 發推特

想必你一定聽過知名的社群平台 Twitter 吧！ twitter 這個詞的原意是「唧唧喳喳的鳥叫聲」，就如同該平台用戶在個人空間所發表的無關緊要的日常文字片段。而原意為「鳥鳴」的動詞 tweet 也引伸成了「發推特」的意思，如：He likes to tweet about his baby boy.「他喜歡在推特上發表關於他兒子的東西。」

• 關於「發文」，你還能這樣說：

She blogged about you.
她寫了關於你的部落格。

Do you like the selfie I posted on my Instagram?
你喜歡我發在 Instagram 上的自拍照嗎？

I'm going to make an Instagram story of it.
我要把它發到 IG 限動上。

blog 寫部落格	selfie 自拍照	post 發佈
Instagram story IG 限時動態		

6. I'll message you later.　我等等發你訊息。

message 發訊息

「發訊息」我們可以說 send me a message，或直接用動詞 message me。在社群平台上，如果要給某人發私訊，我們可以用 direct message 或 private message，也就是我們常見到的 DM 和 PM 兩種縮寫。

* 關於「發訊息」，你還能這樣說：

Direct message me if you have any further inquiry.
如果你還有任何疑問，可以直接私信我。

Drop me a line when you get there.
你到的時候給我發訊息。

Shoot me a text sometime.
有空的時候給我發訊息啊！

direct message 私訊	further 進一步的	inquiry 疑問
drop someone a line 給某人發訊息	shoot someone a text 給某人發訊息	

7. Hello and welcome back to my Youtube channel.

哈囉！歡迎回到我的 Youtube 頻道。

> channel 頻道

目前，社群平台已由原本單純的文字內容演變成了以圖片和影片為主要發表內容的趨勢，這為所有愛秀、敢秀的有才華的創作者提供了一個自由的表演渠道。在這個人人都能成為 Youtuber 的時代，基本的幾句 Youtuber 經典台詞怎能不會說上幾句呢？

• 關於「影音平台」，你還能這樣說：

If you enjoy this video, please remember to give it a like.
如果你喜歡這支影片，記得幫忙按個讚。

If you haven't seen that video, go check that out. I'll put it in the link down below.
如果你還沒看過那支影片，趕快去看。我會把它放在下方的連結。

And as always, I'll see you next time.
好的，那我們下次見囉！

like 按讚	check out 查看	link 連結
as always 如往常一樣		

8. How should I caption this photo?　我這張照片該下什麼標題呢？

> caption 下標題

當大家都在聊 Facebook、Instagram 的時候，你難道不想秀一波英文嗎？比如，當我們在傷腦筋該如何為照片下文案時，我們便能說：How should I caption this photo?「我這張照片該下什麼標題呢？」其中，caption 是「標題」的意思，當動詞用時意思則是「下標題」。另外，當你發現一張照片非常適合發到 IG 上時，你可以說 This is an Instagram worthy photo.「這張照片好適合發 IG。」或直接用 instagrammable 這個詞。最後，一個小提醒：所謂的 FB 和 IG 只有台灣人會這麼說喔！在其他地方，通常是直接說 Facebook 和 Instagram 的，如果你說 FB、IG，對方八成是聽不懂的！

- 關於「網路照片」，你還能這樣說：

This place is so Instagrammable.
這個地方好適合拍照發 IG 喔！

This one is overfiltered.
這張濾鏡也加太多了吧！

You're tagged in this photo.
你被標記在這張照片裡了。

Instagrammable 適合 IG 的	overfiltered 濾鏡過多的	tag 標記

9. Anyone can be an influencer.　人人都能當網紅。

influencer　網紅

隨著網路的民主化，人人都能當網紅的時代也跟著來臨了。然而，作為一名網紅，如果把自己叫做 web red，那可真是丟臉丟到全世界了！所謂的「網紅」其實就是在網路上有影響力的人，因此，在英文中我們會用 influencer 這個詞，另外還有 social media influencer 和 Internet celebrity 的說法。

- 關於「網紅」，你還能這樣說：

His video went viral.
他的影片爆紅了。

She's made quite a name for herself as a Youtuber.
她當 Youtuber 成名了。

He's got 20 million followers on Facebook.
他在臉書上有兩千萬個追蹤人數。

go viral 爆紅	make a name for oneself 成名	Youtuber Youtube 創作者
million 百萬	follower 追蹤者	

10. I feel like Facebook is spying on me. 我感覺臉書好像會監控我。

> feel like 感覺／ spy on 監控

你有過上一秒鐘在網路上下單了一雙鞋，下一秒打開臉書時就發現系統推送了各種鞋子廣告的經驗嗎？沒錯！在網路上，你永遠不知道誰在看著你、誰在聽著你、誰在默默地記錄著你的購物車裡存放了哪些保養品和化妝品。有人說，個資隱私已成了過去式，或許這就是我們享受網路的便利時所該付出的代價吧！

• 關於「網路監控」，你還能這樣說：

It tracks everything I do.
它會記錄我做的所有事情。

Your smartphone might be listening to you.
你的智慧型手機可能在監聽你。

It kinda creeps me out to find that we're all being followed online.
一想到我們都在網路上被跟蹤了就覺得很可怕。

track 跟蹤	smartphone 智慧型手機	creep out 嚇壞
follow 跟蹤	online 線上	

 跟網路有關的慣用語

1. slide into the DM's 私訊某人（通常為陌生人）

哈哈：This girl is so hot! I'm about slide into her DM's.
這個女生好正啊！我要私訊跟她聊一下。

Lyla：I dare you! I double dare you!
你不敢！我笑你不敢！

2. break the Internet　在網路上爆紅

哈哈：Remember when the photo of Matilda broke the Internet?
記得那時候 Matilda 的照片在網路上爆紅嗎？

Lyla：Yeah! Everybody was talking about her at that time.
記得啊！當時每個人都在討論她。

3. work one's fingers to the bone　拚命工作

哈哈：Still working?
還在工作啊？

Lyla：Yeah! My boss kinda expects me to work my fingers to the bone.
對啊！我老闆可能想要我過勞死吧！

4. Facebook stalk　在臉書上跟蹤

哈哈：I Facebook stalked the girl and found out that she's working at the bookstore near my home.
我在臉書上追蹤了那個女孩，發現她在我家附近的書店工作。

Lyla：You pervert!
你變態喔！

5. swipe left　沒興趣

Lyla：Hey! Check out this one! Isn't she cute?
嘿！看一下這個！她還可愛嗎？

哈哈：Well… I'm gonna swipe left on that.
嗯……這個我還好！

第 5 章　哈啦網聊

角色：哈哈（來自台灣）、Lyla（來自美國）

TBH, it's pretty EZ.

OMG! That test pwned me.

NW! U still have a second chance.

Not 4 me. I'm gonna fail.

cya!

OK! g2g!

你看得懂哈哈和 Lyla 的對話嗎？如果可以，那你是個合格的網民了！如果看不懂，本章節來教你關於網路聊天的各種神奇的術語，下次換你用這種異次元語言來嚇唬一下朋友吧！Let's get started!

1. What do you have planned for this weekend?

你這週末要幹嘛？

> plan 計畫

首先來講一下「網友」的說法，如果是指個人在網路上認識的朋友，我們可以說 internet friend「網友」；如果是指在網路上的發表意見、參與討論的網路使用者，我們稱之為 netizen「網民」。而我們在交友軟體上認識的「網友」應該叫做 internet friend 或 online friend。當我們要和網友開啟一段對話時，要怎麼風趣而不失禮貌地破冰呢？一起來看看吧！

• 關於「開啟對話」，你還能這樣說：

How's it going?
你好啊！

Guess who this is.
猜猜我是誰。

That restaurant was really good.
那間餐廳太讚了。

guess 猜	restaurant 餐廳

2. It's his actual bday today. 今天才是他的生日

actual 實際的／bday（birthday） 生日

在學英文的過程中，我們可能已經發現寫作用的書面語和平時交流的口語就已經有非常多的差異了，網聊時，網路用語和日常口語還能讓人覺得它們是兩種不同的語言。主要的原因是網聊時需要非常快的打字速度，因此，很多單詞的拼寫都會縮減，最常見的形式便是將母音省略，或用代表性的子音代替，如：thanks 變 thx、Christmas 變 Xmas、birthday 變 bday、you 變 u、night 變 nite。

• 關於「懶人拼寫法」，你還能這樣說：

Thx, bro!
謝啦！兄弟！

I'll be home in 10 mins.
我再十分鐘就到家了。

Merry Xmas.
聖誕快樂。

Thx（Thanks） 謝謝	bro（brother） 兄弟	mins（minutes） 分鐘
Xmas（Christmas） 聖誕節		

3. Can you w8? 你可以等一下嗎？

w8（wait） 等待

另一種縮減方式是英文字母和數字混用法，如：wait 變 w8、for 變 4、got to go 變 g2g、you too 變 u2 等。有沒有覺得一用起來，屁孩感便大增了呢？

• 關於「火星文」，你還能這樣說：

I don't do this 4 money.
我不是為了錢。

I don't give a f***.
關我什麼事！

2B honest, I couldn't care less.
老實說,我一點都不在意。

1（for）為了	2B（to be） 為了	less 更少

4. np! 沒問題

np（no problem） 沒問題

再介紹一種縮略法 acronym「首字母縮略字」,就是取各個單詞的首字母或代表字母,將其濃縮成一個新詞,如:DM（direct message）表示「私訊」、HBU（How about you?）意思是「那你呢?」、LMAO（laugh my ass off）意思是「笑死我了」。這種縮略法應該是最難懂的了,不過試用看看吧!真的頗容易用上癮的!

• 關於「首字母縮寫」,你還能這樣說：

omg!
天啊!

lol!
笑死!

JK!
開玩笑的!

omg（oh my god）天啊	lol（laugh out loud） 笑死	JK（just kidding）開玩笑的

5. Will have KTV, beer and other entertainment.

會唱 KTV，會有啤酒還有其他娛樂。

> beer　啤酒／ entertainment　娛樂

如同口語英語，網路英語也經常把主詞、Be 動詞或助動詞省略，如：Do you like it? 變 You like it?、I am going to the meeting. 變 Going to the meeting.、It sucks I'll be out of town. 變 Sucks I'll be out of town. 等，管他文法正不正確呢！速度才是終極追求！

- 關於「很愛省略」，你還能這樣說：

OK! Be there soon.
好，我馬上到。

Would be great to have you there.
希望你們都可以去。

Crazy! Not sure how I'll get those in.
太誇張了！不知道要怎麼安排進去。

> **get in**　安排進去

6. Heck yeah boiiii!　好欸！

> boiiii（boy）　男孩

網聊時除非開視訊，不然一般看不到對方的表情和肢體情緒，此時，為了忠實呈現自己的情感，我們就必須善用許多文字形式上的變化。如：yeeeesss!、nooooooo!、sooooo good 等。另一種方式是把要強調的單詞大寫，如：The movie was AMAZING.「那部電影『超讚』的。」

- 關於「誇張表現法」，你還能這樣說：

Nnnnnoooooooooooooooo!
不！！！！！

It was sooo good.
超棒的。

San Francisco is THE BEST.
舊金山超讚的。

San Francisco 舊金山

7. Heck yeah! I got into Berkeley. 好欸！我考進伯克利了！

heck yeah 好欸／get into 進入

除了誇張的拼詞，另一種加強情緒的方式是加入 interjection「感嘆詞」。常見的感嘆詞有：Heck yeah! 表示極度興奮、Wut! 表示震驚、No way! 表示不可置信、Oh my god! 表示震驚或無法接受、hahaha 用來營造輕鬆的語氣。

• 關於「感嘆詞」，你還能這樣說：

Wut! He sent it in the group!?
什麼！他把它傳到群組裡！？

I was trying not to get emotional hahaha.
我有試著要克制自己的情緒，哈哈哈！

No way! You're lying.
不可能！你騙我的吧！？

wut（what） 什麼 | emotional 情緒化的 | lie 說謊

8. I'm in. 我加入。

in 參與的

現代人幾乎都是在社群媒體上揪團辦活動了，當我們收到邀請時，該怎麼表達自己想加入呢？最簡單的說法是 I'm in.「我加入。」或 I'm down.「我加入。」如果一開始拒絕，但事後改變主意想加入時，則可以說 I'm back in the game.「我回鍋了。」

- 關於「加入活動」，你還能這樣說：

I'm down.
我加入。

On board.
我加入。

Yes! Count me in!
好啊！算我一份。

down 參與的	on board 加入……團隊	count 算

9. Fine by me.　我沒問題。

by 由……提出

除了休閒活動外，工作的時候又該如何答應對方的安排或請求呢？一個非常簡潔的說法是 Fine by me. 或 OK by me.「我沒問題。」另外，還有一個相當好用的回覆是 You got it. 意思是「沒問題。」當然，我們也可以說 No problem.。

- 關於「答應某人」，你還能這樣說：

You got it. I will be there.
沒問題，我會到的。

Sure if it'll help.
當然，希望能幫上忙。

I'm ok either way.
我都可以。

You got it. 沒問題。	either 任何一個

10. OK, tell everyone I said hi. I'll chat later. 幫我跟大家問好，之後聊！

> chat 聊天

最後，我們來學學除了發洗澡卡和睡覺卡之外，我們還能如何禮貌地跟對方說再見。一個常用的說法是 Tell everyone I said hi.「幫我跟大家問好。」最後加一句 Talk later.「之後聊。」其中，later 不見得是指「稍後」，在這裡是表示「之後」的意思。

- 關於「結束對話」，你還能這樣說：

Have a great day! Talk later.
保重，之後聊。

Work calls! Talk with you soon.
要去工作了，下次聊喔！

I need to go now. This has been fun.
我得走了，這次跟你聊得很開心。

> call 呼喚

 跟網聊有關的慣用語

1. just sayin' 說說而已

哈哈：What do you think of my presentation?
　　　妳覺得我的報告怎麼樣？

Lyla：It was good, but I think you shouldn't have mentioned the client's name. I'm just sayin'.
　　　很好啊！但我覺得你不應該提到那個客戶的名字，我只是說說我的建議而已啦！

2. shoot someone a text　傳簡訊給某人

哈哈：So when does your train arrive?
　　　妳的火車什麼時候到啊？

Lyla：Not sure. I'll shoot you a text then.
　　　不確定，我到時候給你發訊息。

3. Facebook friend　臉書上的朋友

哈哈：Who's Patrick? You keep mentioning his name recently.
　　　Patrick 是誰啊？妳最近一直提到他的名字。

Lyla：He's just a Facebook friend.
　　　他只是我臉書上的朋友！

4. mouse potato　電腦阿宅

哈哈：Not over yet? You've been chatting for three hours. Stop being a mouse potato.
　　　還沒結束啊？妳已經聊了三個小時了，別再當阿宅啦！

Lyla：This is very important. Stop minding my business.
　　　我們在談重要的事，你別多管閒事。

5. On the Internet, nobody knows you're a dog.
在網路上，沒有人知道你的真實身份。

哈哈：I'm shy. I don't dare to talk with her.
　　　我很害羞，我不敢跟她聊天。

Lyla：On the Internet, nobody knows you're a dog. You can be a totally different person.
　　　在網路上，沒有人知道你真實身份。你可以當一個完全不同的人。

第 6 章　哈啦學校

角色：哈哈（來自台灣）、Lyla（來自美國）

有時候會覺得學生是世界上最幸福的職業，同時也是最辛苦的職業。幸福在於他們單純又豐富的校園生活。學校彷彿提供了一道天然屏障，隔絕了成人世界的現實壓力和煩惱，讓他們能專心致志地完成學業。而說起辛苦的點，也確實是其他職業無法比擬的。工時長、不支薪、各種死線、考試的壓力，對於學生腦力、體力的要求是相當高的。今天，我們就一起來用英語聊聊這辛苦又甜蜜的學校生活吧！

1. I like school because I get to see my friends every day.
我喜歡上學因為我可以每天見到我的朋友。

> get to 得以

求學時期，同儕間的影響之大甚至是超越父母、師長的，很多孩子上學就是為了去見他們的死黨和閨蜜，讀書學習反倒成了次要的事情了。本句「可以見到我朋友」get to see my friends 中的 get to 意思是 have the opportunity to「有⋯⋯的機會」。

• 關於「喜歡上學」，你還能這樣說：

I'm excited about going to Mr. Hendrix's class.
我超喜歡上 Hendrix 老師的課。

One thing I really like about my school is my teachers.
我喜歡我學校的一個點是我的老師們。

Mr. Donald is the best teacher on the face of the earth.
Donald 老師是全宇宙最棒的老師。

| be excited about 期待 | face 表面 | earth 地球 |

2. School sucks. 　學校爛透了！

求學時期，很多家長會說：「當學生很幸福的，等你們長大後就能體會了！」這句話確實不假，但身為學生，身處當下，這句話無法理解的確也是情有可原的啊！很多時候，學校跟職場一樣，充滿著許多討厭的人、事，讓人不禁想說聲：School sucks!「學校爛透了！」這裡的 suck 在口語中是表示「很爛」的意思。或者可以說：I hate school.「我討厭死學校了！」

- 關於「討厭上學」，你還能這樣說：

I don't like that teacher.
我不喜歡那個老師。

Nobody likes me at school.
學校沒有一個人喜歡我。

Can I stay home from school tomorrow?
我明天可以不去學校嗎？

stay　待在

3. In the UK, school starts at nine and finishes at half three.
在英國，學生九點上學，三點半下課。

half three　三點半

描述學校作息時，為了表示習慣性、表定的事情，我們一般會用「現在簡單式」。如：School starts at nine and finishes at half three.「學生九點上學，三點半下課。」其中，「三點半」一般我們會說 half past three，然而在平時的口語中，說 half three 其實就可以囉！

- 關於「學校作息」，你還能這樣說：

We have a good two-hour lunch break in between.
我們中間有兩個多小時的午休。

The second period in the afternoon is a self-study time.
下午的第二節是自習課。

Here in California, schools can start at 8:30-ish depending on the grade you're currently in.
在加州這裡，學校大概八點半左右開始上課，看你目前是幾年級會有所不同。

good 超過	lunch break 午休	in between 中間
period 節	self-study 自習	California 加州
depend on 取決於	grade 年級	currently 目前
-ish 大約		

4. We are going to run a Monday schedule tomorrow.
明天我們走的是星期一的課表。

run 執行

有時候，學校因為補課或調課等原因，課務可能不會照正常的行事曆走，比如：星期五可能會上星期一的課表，而這種情形在英文中要怎麼表達呢？「上星期一的課表」我們會說：run a Monday schedule，其中 run 是「執行」的意思；或 Is today considered a Thursday?「今天是走星期四的課表嗎？」而「停課」是 no school，「補課」則是 make-up day。

- 關於「週課表」，你還能這樣說：

There will be no school on Friday.
這週五不用上學。

We only have three days this week.
我們這個星期只上三天課。

This Sunday will be a make-up day for Labor Day holiday.
這週日要補勞動節假期的課。

school 上學	make-up 補	Labor Day 勞動節

5. Mandarin will be switched to the first period.

中文課會調到第一節。

> Mandarin 中文／ switch 調換

「調課」的英文是 switch。「英文課和中文課調課」我們會說：English is switched with Chinese. 或更簡單的 English becomes Chinese, and Chinese becomes English.。「中文課調到第一節」Mandarin will be switched to the first period.。「第三節還是化學課」The third period remains Chemistry.。

- 關於「課程調動」，你還能這樣說：

Physics is rescheduled to Tuesday afternoon.
物理課調到星期二下午。

This Friday's Global Perspective is cancelled.
這星期五的全球視野課取消了。

Mr. Roberts will take over Shawn's math.
Roberts 老師會接手 Shawn 老師的數學課。

reschedule 調動	global 全球的	perspective 視角
cancel 取消	take over 接手	

6. Attention! 注意聽！

> attention 專注

對於畢業許久的人來說，老師的經典語錄想必很令人懷念吧！特別是那些甜蜜的訓斥，讓人不禁想重回教室再被洗禮一次呢！

- 關於「老師語錄（一）」，你還能這樣說：

Do I have your attention?
可以注意聽我說嗎？

Any questions so far?
有沒有問題？

OK! Class! It's time for break.
好！下課了！

| attention 注意力 | so far 到目前為止 | break 休息 |

7. Calm down and be quiet, or I'll give you detention.
安靜！否則我送你去留校察看。

calm down 冷靜下來／detention 留校察看

長大後，有些人可能也當了老師，當他們在教育學生時，除了發現自己也變成滿嘴碎碎唸的煩人師長之外，甚至還承襲了自己老師的口頭禪，而且發現這些金句竟然還挺好用的呢！像是：You better be quiet, or I'll call your parents.「你最好安靜，否則我就打電話給你爸媽。」

• 關於「老師語錄（二）」，你還能這樣說：

No running in the hallway.
走廊上不要奔跑。

Raise your hand before you speak.
要講話的舉手。

Don't worry! It's not gonna be graded.
別擔心，這個不會算成績。

| hallway 走廊 | raise 舉起 | grade 算成績 |

8. Can you pass the paint please? 可以把顏料傳過來給我嗎？

pass 傳遞／paint 顏料

「傳紙條」、「借東西」、「佔位」、「點名」，除了這些之外，你記憶中還有什麼經典的學生語錄呢？其中，「傳」這個動作的英文是 pass，「傳閱」則是pass around。

- 關於「同學語錄（一）」，你還能這樣說：

Can I borrow your correction tape?
我可以借用你的修正帶嗎？

Can you save me a seat in the last row please?
你可以在最後一排幫我佔個位子嗎？

Has the teacher done the roll call yet?
老師點名了嗎？

borrow 借	correction tape 修正帶	save 保存
seat 座位	row 排	roll call 點名

9. Bye! Mrs. Cole. 老師再見！

Mrs. 女士

稱呼老師，我們一般會用 Mr.、Ms. 或 Mrs. 加老師的姓。或者我們也可以說 Teacher ＋姓「……老師」。

- 關於「同學語錄（二）」，你還能這樣說：

See you at school.
學校見！

What are you doing after school?
你放學後要做什麼？

Will this be in the test?
這個會考嗎？

after school 放學後

10. Wake up! Honey! Or you'll be late for school!

親愛的起床了！不然你上學要遲到了！

> honey 親愛的／ be late for school 上學遲到

最後，我們來學學「家長的經典語錄」。看看歐美家長和亞洲家長的說法有什麼異同。如果你是家長，這幾句可以學起來幫孩子創造一些英語情境噢！

• 關於「家長語錄」，你還能這樣說：

Have a great day! Learn something!
今天過得開心喔！好好學習喔！

How was school?
今天上學怎麼樣？

Why don't you tell me what you learned at school today?
你要不要告訴我你今天在學校學了些什麼啊？

> **why don't you…** 你要不要……

 跟學校有關的慣用語

1. class clown　搗蛋鬼

哈哈：Believe it or not, I used to be a class clown back in the day.
相信嗎？我以前上課時曾是個搗蛋鬼呢！

Lyla：I very much believe it. Without a doubt.
我非常相信，毫不懷疑。

2. play hooky　翹課

Lyla：Were you a naughty kid when you were in school?
你上學的時候很調皮嗎？

哈哈：Yes! I remember when I got caught playing hooky in middle school, my mom was so angry.

超調皮！我記得我中學的時候翹課被抓，我媽媽超生氣！

3. drop out 休學

哈哈：Why did we have to work so hard before? Steve Jobs dropped out of college and became the father of Apple.

我們以前何必那麼辛苦唸書呢？賈伯斯大學休學，然後就創辦了蘋果呢！

Lyla：Well…you are not exactly Steve Jobs.

問題是你不是賈伯斯啊！

4. put oneself through school 自行負擔學費

哈哈：Did you have to put yourself through college?

妳之前需要自己負擔學費嗎？

Lyla：Yes. I was working three different jobs in college to pay for my tuition.

要啊！我當時做了三份工作，就是為了付我的學費。

5. draw a blank 眼神放空

哈哈：How was your weekend?

週末過得如何？

Lyla：...Sorry! I was drawing a blank. What was that you said again?

……對不起！我剛剛出神了，你剛剛説什麼？

第 7 章　哈啦讀書

角色：哈哈（來自台灣）、Lyla（來自美國）

讀書是每個人成長的必經過程。雖然不是每個人在求學階段都能明白讀書的目的或領悟讀書的樂趣，但十幾年的義務教育或多或少對我們都造成了一定的影響，回憶起來總是甜蜜的回憶。不管對你來說是過去式還是進行式，今天我們都一起來學習關於讀書的英語對話吧！

1. I'm a college freshman student.　我是一位大一生。

> college　大學／freshman　大一

相信大家都知道「大學」有兩種說法：college 和 university。college 是指「四年制的大學」，而 university 則包含大學和研究所。但在一般的口語裡，人們一般較常說 college。

大學四個年級的說法分別是：freshman「大一」、sophomore「大二」、junior「大三」和 senior「大四」。而表達自己是大一生最簡單的說法是：I'm a college freshman student. 或 I'm in my freshman year of college.。其他表達法還有：I've got two more years to go.「我還有兩年畢業。」或 I'm in year 10 of high school「我現在就讀高中十年級。」

• 關於「正在就讀」，你還能這樣說：

I'm in my final year. I'll graduate in June.
今年是我最後一年，我今年六月畢業。

I study at high school.
我現在讀高中。

I'm currently taking a gap year.
我現在是空檔年。

final　最後的	graduate　畢業	currently　目前
gap year　空檔年		

2. I'm doing a PhD in biochemistry. 我現在在讀生物化學的博士。

> PhD 博士學位／biochemistry 生物化學

當別人問到：What are you studying?「你是唸什麼的？」或 What's your major?「你主修什麼？」時，我們回答時可以用的動詞有 do、study、pursue 和 work toward。比如「我在讀……的博士。」我們可以說：I'm doing a PhD in...、I'm studying a PhD in...、I am pursuing a PhD in... 和 I'm working toward a PhD in...。

- 關於「攻讀學位」，你還能這樣說：

I'm studying to become a doctor.
我在讀醫學院。

I'm currently pursuing my Bachelor's degree in Singapore.
我目前在新加坡攻讀學士學位。

I'm studying at the University of Bristol for a Master's degree in English literature.
我現在在布里斯托大學讀英國文學碩士學位。

pursue 追求	Bachelor's degree 學士學位	Singapore 新加坡
Bristol 布里斯托	Master's degree 碩士學位	literature 文學

3. I'm taking a class on Cross Cultural Communication with Dr. Yu. 我在上余教授的跨文化溝通。

> take 上……課／cross 跨越的／cultural 文化的／communication 溝通

大學每到學期初時，最常討論的話題就是「選課」了。「選課」我們可以說：add one's class、take one's class 或 take a class on ＋學科＋ with ＋老師。如果要表達「我上過……的課」，我們可以說：I had...before.。比如：I had him for another class.「我上過他的另一門課。」

- 關於「選課（一）」，你還能這樣說：

I started taking a Spanish class.
我開始上西班牙語課了。

I signed up for a French class.
我報名了一堂法語課。

Last term, I took psychology with Mrs. Woodfield.
上學期我上了 Woodfield 老師的心理學。

Spanish 西班牙語	sign up 報名	French 法語
term 學期	psychology 心理學	

4. Dr. Wayne's classes always fill up fast.
Wayne 教授的課老是很快就會被選完。

fill up 加滿

「熱門課」英文是 popular class 或 popular course。如果某位老師的課很熱門，很快就會爆滿，我們可以說：fill up fast。而「營養學分」或「涼課」的英文則是 easy As「很好拿的 A 等」或 cake course。

- 關於「選課（二）」，你還能這樣說：

Matt is a tough grader. You gotta work very hard.
Matt 打分很嚴格的，你得非常努力。

I'm looking for easy As anyway.
反正我也是在找涼課選。

I took 32 credits this semester.
我這學期修了三十二個學分。

tough grader 打分嚴格的人	gotta 必須	easy As 很容易過關的課
credit 學分	semester 學期	

5. My favorite subject is math.　我最喜歡的科目是數學。

subject 學科／math 數學

如果要說「我最喜歡的科目是⋯」，我們可以說：My favorite subject is always... 或 ...is always my favorite subject.。而「擅長的科目」和「不擅長的科目」分別是 strong subject 和 weak subject。

• 關於「學科喜好」，你還能這樣說：

Since I was a kid, history has been my favorite subject.
從我小時候，歷史一直是我最愛的科目。

I'm afraid of English.
我很怕英語。

I can't decide what my favorite subject is.
我不知道我最喜歡的科目是什麼。

history 歷史	afraid 害怕的	decide 決定

6. I gotta go home and hit the books.　我得回家讀書了。

hit the books 讀書

hit 這個動詞在英文口語中非常常見，通常是指「去到」或「接觸」的意思。如：hit the books「讀書」、hit the road「上路」、hit the sack「睡覺」、hit the gym「上健身房」、hit the library「去圖書館」等。除此之外，還可以說：pound the books。

• 關於「K 書」，你還能這樣說：

I'd better go study.
我得去讀書了。

You better study up.
你最好好好讀書。

I am invited to a study session.
我被邀請去參加一個讀書會。

had better 最好	entire 整個	study up 好好讀書
study session 讀書會		

7. I've been studying like crazy. 我一直超認真地在讀書。

like crazy 使勁地

I've been studying like crazy.「我一直超認真地在讀書。」這個句子用的時態是「現在完成進行式」，表示從過去到現在一直在進行的動作，通常中文會翻成「一直……」。like crazy 則是一個口語中常用來表示「程度很強烈」或「不受控制」的意思。如：work like crazy「瘋狂工作」、drive like crazy「亂開車」等。

- 關於「認真讀書」，你還能這樣說：

I can see she's been putting in a lot of effort.
我看得出來她最近一直很努力。

He's trying really hard.
他很用功。

There's a lot of coffee in me right now.
我喝了很多咖啡。

effort 努力

8. I can never focus while I'm studying.

我讀書的時候根本沒辦法專心。

focus 專心

就和早起一樣，讀書最難的部份是下定決心要開始的那一刻。然而，不想讀書的理由總是有千千萬萬種。現在，我們就來學學如何用英文耍賴不讀書吧！

• 關於「不想讀書」，你還能這樣說：

I just want to be lazy.
我只想犯懶。

I don't want to study.
我不想讀書。

My exams are coming but I don't feel like studying.
快要考試了，但我不想唸書。

lazy 懶惰的	exam 考試	feel like 想要

9. I think I might have to pull an all-nighter.

我覺得我可能需要開夜車了。

might 可能／ pull an all-nighter 熬夜工作

不管是準備考試還是做報告，學生的共性就是：通通都拖到最後一秒鐘，直到火燒屁股了才開始緊張焦慮。此時，我們可以怎麼表達我們的心情呢？

• 關於「臨時抱佛腳」，你還能這樣說：

I haven't even started studying.
我根本還沒開始讀書。

My mid-term is coming up. I have to cram for it.
我快期中考了，我要惡補一下。

I always study at the last minute and it actually works.

我總是到最後關頭才開始讀書，而且這樣其實還蠻有效的。

| mid-term 期中考 | come up 來臨 | cram 惡補 |
| at the last minute 最後關頭 | work 有效 | |

10. When I study, I need complete silence. 我讀書的時候需要非常安靜。

complete 完全的／ silence 安靜

雖說只要有心，到哪都能讀書。但不可否認的是，環境對人的影響還是很大的。有些人需要完全安靜的空間，有些人卻能一邊聽重金屬音樂一邊算數學題。關於自己的讀書習慣，我們可以怎麼表達呢？

- 關於「讀書習慣」，你還能這樣說：

I am a multitasker.
我習慣多工處理。

I usually study with music.
我通常會一邊聽音樂一邊讀書。

I've booked a study room in Beacon House.
我在 Beacon House 預定了一間自習室。

| multitasker 多工處理的人 | book 預訂 | study room 自習室 |

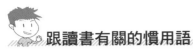

1. know one's stuff　精通自己的專業

哈哈：I think Jerry is so knowledgeable. He really knows his stuff.
我覺得 Jerry 好博學啊！他真的懂好多。

Lyla：Not to me. I think there's a difference between being
knowledgeable and being a bookworm.
我可不這麼認為。在我看來，博學和書呆子還是有區別的。

2. study animal　刻苦讀書的人

哈哈：I can't go out tonight. I have to study for my final.
我今晚不能出去了，我得準備我的期末考。

Lyla：Haha! Everybody turns into a study animal at the end of the
semester.
每個人學期末都突然變得好用功啊！

3. cake course　涼課

哈哈：Are you adding Helen's class? The biggest cake course ever!
妳要選 Helen 的課嗎？史上最涼的課欸！

Lyla：I wanted to, but it's full already.
我想選，但已經滿了。

4. plug away　用功讀書、工作

哈哈：How's your project going so far?
妳的專案寫得怎麼樣啊？

Lyla：Not even half way through. Still need to keep plugging away.
一半都還沒到呢！還需要繼續努力。

5. burn the midnight oil　挑燈夜讀

哈哈：I totally forgot I have an exam tomorrow.
我完全忘記我明天有考試了。

Lyla：Seems like you'll need to burn the midnight oil.
看來你得挑燈夜讀了。

第 8 章　哈啦考試

角色：哈哈（來自台灣）、Lyla（來自美國）

考試想必是所有人的夢魘吧！從小到大，我們都經歷過大大小小的考試，甚至連畢業進入職場之後，仍然需要面對各種專業或執照考試。看來不管是西方還是東方社會，考試都如影隨形，彷彿是堂鍛鍊心理素質的人生必修課。今天，不管是要吐苦水還是話當年，都先來學學如何用英語哈啦考試吧！

1. I'm so stressed out about my final.　我期末考壓力好大。

> stressed out　壓力大／ final　期末考

「考試」的英文有：test、exam 和 quiz。其中，test 是指廣義的考試或測評，除了指學科考試外，還可以是生活中的各種測試，比如：eye test「視力檢測」、blood test「血液檢測」、driving test「駕照考試」等；exam 較為正式且全面，通常是學習的階段性檢測；而 quiz 是指小考，通常是非正式而隨機的。學校的期中考和期末考分別叫 midterm exam 和 final exam，通常會縮稱為 midterm 和 final。「準備考試」則可以說：study for an exam 或 cram for an exam。其中，cram 有「臨時抱佛腳」的意思。

[註]：各種考試的英文：entrance exam 入學考試／ proficiency test 能力檢測／ placement exam 分班考試／ qualifying exam 資格考試／ comprehensive exam 綜合測試／ aptitude test 性向測驗／ intelligence test 智力測驗／ pop quiz 課堂小考／ oral test 口試／ written test 筆試

• 關於「準備考試」，你還能這樣說：

I was up late studying for the midterm.
我熬夜準備期中考。

To up my grades, my mother sent me to this intensive study program.
為了提升我的成績，我媽媽送我去上一個強化課程。

I'm cramming for tomorrow's test.
我在準備明天的考試。

up 醒著的	midterm 期中考	up 提升
intensive 高強度的	program 課程	cram 填鴨式學習

2. What's going to be on? 要考什麼？

> on 出現

「考試要考什麼？」我們可以說：What's going to be on the test? 或簡化成：What's going to be on? 另外，也可以用 cover「包括」這個字，如：What's going to be covered?「要考什麼？」。而「考試的範圍」有：comprehensive test「無範圍考試」或 cumulative test「累積範圍考試」，也就是前次考過的還會再出現。

- 關於「考試範圍」，你還能這樣說：

What's going to be covered on the test?
這次考試要考什麼？

What's the scope?
範圍是什麼？

It's gonna be a comprehensive test.
這次考試是沒有範圍的。

cover 包含	scope 範圍	comprehensive 全面的

3. I took the test a few years ago. 我幾年前考過這個考試。

> take 參加

「參加考試」千萬不能說 join the test 喔！正確的說法應該是 take the test 或 do the test。如果你是老師，「給學生考試」則是用 give a test。

- 關於「參加考試」，你還能這樣說：

We have a big test tomorrow.
我們明天有一場很重要的考試。

I was doing my history finals.
我當時在考歷史期末考。

The teacher gave us a quiz in English.

老師給我了們一次英文小考。

quiz 小考

4. How did the test go?　考試考得怎麼樣？

go 進行

考完試，問別人「考得如何？」我們可以說：How did it go?「考得怎樣？」、Was it hard?「很難嗎？」、Was it on things you studied?「考的都是你讀到的內容嗎？」第一句的動詞 go 表示「進行」的意思。

- 關於「考得如何」，你還能這樣說：

How was the test?

考試考得怎麼樣？

How did you do on the test?

你考試考得怎麼樣？

Do you think you did well?

你覺得考得還好嗎？

well 好

5. I got something around the average.　我的分數大概在平均分左右。

average 平均

一般說考試「得幾分」，我們會用 get 這個動詞。如：I got an eighty.「我考了八十分。」但通常不會說：I got eighty points.，因為 point「分數」通常是指在課堂上表現好而得到的分數。

- 關於「考試成績」，你還能這樣說：

I got seventy something.

我考了七十幾分。

Most students got ninety plus.
大部分的學生都考了九十幾分。

I got below 60.
我考六十分以下。

plus 加	below 以下

6. Aced it.　考得不錯！

> ace　考得好

考試考得好，我們便可眉飛色舞地説：I aced it! 或 I nailed it. 表示「我考得很好！」如果説是「輕鬆過關」，我們會説：I sail through the test.；如果是「勉強過關」則是：I scraped through the test.。

• 關於「考得好」，你還能這樣說：

Easy-peasy.
超簡單。

At least I passed my own bar.
至少我有達到我自己的標準。

I managed to scrape through my finals.
我好不容易通過了期末考。

easy-peasy 非常簡單	at least 至少	pass one's own bar 通過自己的標準
manage to 設法	scrape through 勉強通過	finals 期末考

7. I bombed it.　我考砸了。

> bomb　考砸

萬一不幸考砸了，英文也有很多種說法的！比如：I failed it.「我考不及格。」、I didn't score high in that one.「我那科考得不高。」、I did poorly.「考得很糟。」、I did terribly.「考得很差。」或 I bombed it.「我考砸了。」、I messed up.「我考壞了。」

- 關於「考得不好」，你還能這樣說：

The reading killed me.
那篇閱讀難倒我了。

I did not do well. I lost fifteen points from the listening.
我考得不好，我聽力就扣了十五分。

I did very poorly. I think I'm going to flunk this semester.
我考得很差。我覺得我這學期要被當掉了。

kill　殺死	point　分	poorly　差地
flunk　被當	semester　學期	

8. She is at the top of her class.　她算是班上頂尖的。

> top　頂部

歐美學校的考試成績一般都不是用具體的分數，而是用 grade「等第」來分級，如：A、B、C 三等制。而學校或班級的排名也都是採取前百分之幾的排法。因此，如果一個學生在班上排名是最靠前的，我們可以說他是 at the top of the class「排名頂尖」，相反的則是 at the bottom of the class「排名墊底」。

- 關於「成績優異」，你還能這樣說：

He has the best grades in his class.
他的成績是班上最好的。

He's always the top ten percent of his class.
他一直是班上的前百分之十。

I'm ranked number one in the school.

我是全校第一名。

grade 成績	percent 百分比	rank 排名

9. The teacher is gonna explain the test today.

老師今天會講解考卷。

explain 解釋／ test 考卷

「講解考卷」我們可以說：explain the test 或 go over the test；「批改考卷」是 mark the test 或 grade the test；「發還考卷」則是 return the test。

• 關於「講解考卷」，你還能這樣說：

The teacher will go over the test next week.

老師下週會檢討作業。

When will the test be returned?

考卷什麼時候會發還？

It's still being graded.

考卷還在批改。

go over 講解	return 發還	grade 評分

10. Emma was caught cheating on the math test.

Emma 考數學的時候作弊被抓。

cheat 作弊

「被抓到……」我們可以用這個句型：be caught V-ing。因此，「被抓到作弊」就是 be caught cheating。如果是「當場被抓到」，還可以加上 red handed，彷彿手上還沾滿鮮血般證據確鑿。而作弊的「小抄」英文則是 crib sheet 或 cheat sheet。「傳小抄」則是 pass the cheat sheet。

- 關於「考試作弊」，你還能這樣說：

I copied his answers.
我抄他的答案的。

He cribbed the answers from his friend.
他抄他朋友的答案的。

He brought a cheat sheet to the exam.
他帶小抄去考試。

crib 抄襲	cheat sheet 小抄

 跟考試有關的慣用語

1. sail through the test　考試輕鬆過關

哈哈：So how did the test go?
　　　考試考得如何啊？

Lyla：Sailed through it. I even slept for a while before I turned it in.
　　　輕鬆過關，我交卷前還睡了一下呢！

2. go easy on　放水

哈哈：Was it hard?
　　　考試很難嗎？

Lyla：Too easy! I think Mr. Flinch went easy on us.
　　　我覺得 Flinch 老師放水了。

3. fingers crossed for you　祝順利

哈哈：There's a big test tomorrow which I have to get an A on.
　　　明天有一場重要的考試，我必須考到 A 才行。

Lyla：Fingers crossed for you.
　　　祝你順利喔！

4. pass with flying colors　輕鬆過關

哈哈：Did you pass the test?
　　　妳考試過了嗎？

Lyla：Yes! With flying colors!
　　　當然！輕鬆過關！

5. in the bag　穩當；非常確定能成功

哈哈：Looks like you have to get an A to pass.
　　　看樣子妳必須得拿到 A 才能過關欸！

Lyla：That's in the bag. I don't even have to try.
　　　輕而易舉！我根本不用費力。

第 9 章 哈啦作業

角色：哈哈（來自台灣）、Lyla（來自美國）

My dog ate my homework!「我的狗吃了我的作業！」你有沒有聽過這麼瞎的不交作業的理由呢？作業可說是人人都不愛，但又不得不面對！講到寫作業、交報告，相信很多人都有很多心酸血淚史吧！想知道什麼是 procrastinate、proofreading、plagiarism 是什麼嗎？一起來學學交作業的英文句子吧！

1. I'm done for today. But I'll kill it tomorrow.
我今天就寫到這，明天一定把它完成！

> done 完成的／ kill 完成

「我做完了。」除了可以說 I finished.，也可以用 I'm done. 來表示。如果是整份工作都完成了，可以說：It's done.。另外，還可以用 kill 來表示「完成」，通常是帶有強烈的決心的意味。

• 關於「奮力寫作業」，你還能這樣說：

I sat up all night writing my assignment.
我通宵寫作業。

I've done nothing but do my homework during the past four days.
我這四天來除了做作業之外什麼都沒做。

We've been working around the clock to get our assignments done.
我們一直馬不停蹄地在寫作業。

| sit up all night 通宵 | around the clock 日以繼夜 |

第9章 哈啦作業

083

2. We kinda needed a change of environment to get our work done. 我們需要換個環境來把我們的工作完成。

> environment 環境

change of environment 表示「換個環境」，也可以說：change of scenery。寫作業遇到瓶頸時，嘗試換個環境，創造點新鮮感，說不定能大幅提高工作效率喔！另外，get our work done 也可以說成 get done our work，也就是 finish our work 的另一種說法。

- 關於「寫作業的過程（一）」，你還能這樣說：

Shhh! I'm doing my work here! I need to concentrate.
噓！我在做作業！我需要專心！

It's so hard to keep my eyes open! I'm falling asleep!
眼睛睜著都好難啊！我快睡著了！

I'm ready to take a five-minute break!
我要休息五分鐘。

| concentrate 專心 | fall asleep 睡著 | break 休息 |

3. I usually work best in the company of others.
我通常有人陪伴時工作效率最好。

> company 陪伴

company 除了「公司」之外還有「陪伴」的意思。比如：I really enjoy your company.「有你的陪伴我真的很開心。」而「在……的陪伴下」我們可以說：in the company of…。有些人就是喜歡「聚眾」寫作業，有些人則是習慣單槍匹馬，你是屬於哪一種呢？

- 關於「寫作業的過程（二）」，你還能這樣說：

I've eaten, breathed and slept my assignment.
我連吃飯、呼吸、睡覺都在做我的作業。

I gotta make sure my homework space is free of distractions.

我必須確保我寫作業的地方是沒有任何干擾的。

Something is better than nothing. Just keep at it!

有了總比沒有好。就繼續做吧！

breathe 呼吸	space 空間	free 沒有的
distraction 干擾	keep at 堅持	

4. The deadline is the twentieth. Don't flake.

截止日是二十號，別出包了！

deadline 截止日／flake 出錯

deadline 就是我們直譯的「死線」，也就是「截止日期」。相關的搭配語有：set the deadline「設定截止日期」、meet the deadline「在截止日期前完成」、miss the deadline「錯過截止日期」、work to a tight deadline「工作時間很緊」等。flake 原指「碎片」、「剝落」，在口語中還可以表示「出包」或「未能完成工作」的意思。

• 關於「進度落後」，你還能這樣說：

I'm already behind on my ALT assignment.

我 ALT 的作業進度已經落後了。

I'm not even halfway through.

我連一半都還沒完成。

I should stop procrastinating and get down to my assignments.

我不該再拖拖拉拉，要開始寫作業了。

behind 落後	assignment 作業	halfway 一半
through 通過	procrastinate 拖延	get down to 開始做

5. Can you help me out with a question?　你可以教我一題嗎？

> help out　幫忙

help out 表示「幫忙」。help me out 則是「幫我一下」。搭配的介系詞用 with。通常問別人問題之前，我們會先問一下：You got a minute?「你有空嗎？」、Quick question.「我想問一下。」、Just a quick question.「我想問一下。」等。

- 關於「尋求幫助」，你還能這樣說：

Can you share your answers with me?
你可以給我看一下你的答案嗎？

I may need a little help here. I don't see how it works.
我需要一點幫助，我不懂這題為什麼會這樣。

Hi! Are you free at the moment? I've got a quick question for you.
嗨！你現在有空嗎？我有一個小問題。

> work　進行

6. Oh my God! This is never gonna end.　天啊！這永遠都做不完！

> end　結束

你是否曾有過那種作業、報告堆積如山，永遠都看不到終點的絕望感呢？這種情況，你就可以說：This is never gonna end!「這永遠都做不完啊！」

- 關於「作業寫不完」，你還能這樣說：

I'm never gonna finish this!
我永遠都做不完。

What if I get expelled for this? My mom's gonna kill me.
我因為這個被退學了怎麼辦？我媽會殺了我的。

I can't do this! I give up!
我做不了！

| expel 開除 | kill 殺 | give up 放棄 |

7. I'm off the hook now.　我解脫了。

off the hook　解脫

hook 是「掛鉤」，off the hook 則好像是從掛鉤上解脫下來的感覺，表示「解脫了」。也可以說：Free at last!「終於解脫了！」、Finally!!!「終於啊！」

• <u>關於「交作業」</u>，你還能這樣說：

I've turned it in.
我已經交了。

It's so liberating!
感覺解脫了！

I'm finally done with my assignment!
我作業終於寫完了！

turn in　繳交	liberating 令人感到自由的	done　完成
assignment　作業		

8. Chill! I still have the whole weekend to complete it.
別擔心！我還有整個週末可以完成它。

chill 放輕鬆／ whole 整個／ complete 完成

chill 這個字最近十分流行，它可以當動詞，表示「冷卻」、「放輕鬆」；當名詞，表示「寒冷」、「感冒」；當形容詞，表示「一派輕鬆的」。下次讓別人「放輕鬆」、「別擔心」時，除了說：Don't worry!、Take it easy!、Relax! 之外，試試看這個字 Chill!

• <u>關於「拖延症患者」</u>，你還能這樣說：

Why the rush? It can't take too long to do.
幹嘛這麼趕呢？它不可能花我太多時間的。

I'll do it tomorrow.
我明天再做吧！

I'll start after I finish the last episode.

我最後一集看完再開始。

take 花費	episode 集

9. I am gonna ask for an extension.　我要申請遲交。

> extension 延展

關於交作業，有些事情是必須知道的。比如，在英國很多大學都允許學生因為個人原因，比如：小到和哥哥吵架心情不好，大到生病，而遲交作業。「申請遲交」的英文是 apply for an extension 或 ask for an extension。「延遲申請」則叫 deadline extension。

・關於「交作業大小事」，你還能這樣說：

Can you do a proofreading for me?

你可以幫我校稿嗎？

That's plagiarism!

那算是抄襲欸！

When will our grades be visible?

我們的成績何時出來？

proofreading 校稿	plagiarism 抄襲	grade 成績
visible 可見的		

10. I stress over my homework a lot.　我經常煩惱我的作業問題。

> stress 煩惱

為了減輕學生的學業負擔，近年來很多人在鼓吹取消家庭作業，也有聽說很多教師已不再安排學生的回家作業，改在課堂上完成，這類的新聞總能引起正反兩極的評價。確實，家庭作業的存留是道值得深究的辯題，對於這個議題，你的看法是什麼呢？

- 關於「該不該有作業」，你還能這樣說：

I think homework should be banned cause it takes up too much of our time after school.
我認為作業應該被取消，因為它佔據我們太多的課後時間了。

A little homework is good cause it keeps you sharp and helps you retain what you learn.
一點點作業是好的，因為它能讓你思緒更敏銳，並幫助你記得學過的東西。

We should make sure homework is balanced with enough play time.
我們應該平衡好作業和玩樂的時間。

ban 禁止	take up 佔據	sharp 敏銳的
retain 保留	balance 使平衡	

 跟作業有關的慣用語

1. My dog ate my homework.　狗吃了我的作業。

哈哈：Mr. Thompson, my dog ate my homework.
　　　Thompson 老師，我家的狗吃了我的作業。

Mr. Thompson：Again? I'm tired of your lame excuse.
　　　　　　　又來了？我受夠你的爛藉口了。

2. do one's homework　做了準備

哈哈：Are you ready for this interview?
　　　妳這次面試準備好了嗎？

Lyla：Yes. I've done my homework! Can't wait to begin.
　　　準備好了，我這次做足了準備，我等不及要開始了。

3. goof off　遊手好閒不工作

哈哈：Why are you still goofing off and not doing your work?
　　　妳怎麼還在晃來晃去，不工作呢？

Lyla：I'm not goofing off. I'm looking for inspiration.
　　　我沒在亂晃，我在找靈感。

4. make the grade　達到標準

哈哈：Why are you moping?
　　　妳怎麼悶悶不樂的？

Lyla：I didn't make the grade. I have to do it all over again.
　　　我沒有達到標準，必須從頭來過了。

5. hit the bottleneck　遇到瓶頸

哈哈：How's your video going so far?
　　　妳的影片拍得如何啊？

Lyla：I think I'm hitting the bottleneck. I may need some help.
　　　我覺得我可能遇到瓶頸了，我需要一點幫助。

第10章 哈啦面試

角色：哈哈（來自台灣）、Lyla（來自美國）

面試很可怕、很令人頭疼，世界上大概找不到有人是喜歡面試的吧！然而，從小到大我們都不得不面對各種面試，包含：學校面試、項目面試、工作面試甚至到婚姻面試。本章節，我們要談的主要是針對工作的 job interview「求職面試」，我們會用 interviewee「受面試者」的角度來聊聊一場面試從頭到尾該如何得體應對、見招拆招。西裝領帶穿起來，進場面試囉！

1. I'm stressing out about this interview. 我好緊張這次的面試啊！

> stress out 緊張／ interview 面試

首先，第一步當然是找朋友抱怨、發洩一下啦！面試前的各種緊張、焦慮，甚至由其引發的生理現象該怎麼說呢？「緊張」我們可以用 stress 這個詞，基本有兩種說法：I'm stressing out. 或 I'm stressed out.「我好緊張。」而由 stress 引伸出來的形容詞 stressful「壓力大的」則是用來形容事物令人緊張，比如：That is so stressful!「它讓人壓力好大！」另外，「焦慮」的英文則是 anxiety，如：I understand your anxiety.「我能理解你的焦慮。」形容詞是 anxious，如：I'm anxious about the interview.「我對這場面試感到很焦慮。」有些人面試前會因太緊張而腸胃不適，這種時候就叫 have the runs「拉肚子」啦！

• 關於「面試前」，你還能這樣說：

This is so nerve-wracking.
神經好緊繃啊！

I'm gonna have a panic attack at the interview.
我面試的時候要恐慌發作了。

I've been there. I know preparing for an interview can be stressful.
我以前也這樣過，所以我知道準備面試真的讓人壓力很大。

nerve-wracking 神經緊繃的	panic attack 恐慌發作	prepare 準備
stressful 壓力大的		

2. It's my pleasure to meet you.　很高興見到你。

> pleasure 榮幸

開始面試了！通常面試官在正式開始前會先和你寒暄閒聊幾句，這個環節我們叫 small talk「閒聊」，目的是幫助受試者緩和緊張情緒，營造較輕鬆的氛圍。以下是幾個面試官常用的 small talk 句子，下方則是相應的回答。

Hello. I'm Shawn Smith. Thanks so much for coming in.
您好，我是 Shawn Smith，感謝您前來。

How are you doing?
你好嗎？

Did you have any trouble finding this place?
我們這裡會很難找嗎？

• 關於「閒聊」，你還能這樣說：

Thanks so much for meeting with me.
感謝你安排跟我見面。

I'm doing great! How are you doing?
我很好，你好嗎？

No. The office isn't too difficult to find.
不會！這個辦公室不難找。

| meet with… 與……見面 | office 辦公室 |

3. I studied at the University of Birmingham and graduated in 2020 with a degree in marketing.

我之前在伯明漢大學讀行銷學，於二零二零年畢業。

> university 大學／ Birmingham 伯明翰／ graduate 畢業／ degree 學位／ marketing 行銷

當面試官説：Tell me about yourself.「介紹一下你自己。」時，通常就是要你做一段簡短地自我介紹，這時最基本的做法就是從自己的教育背景説起。但這當然不是要你介紹你的國中老師多嚴格或讀過哪所明星高中之類的上古史，而是和你求職最相關的大學或研究所時期，並講述一下這些時期的所學和經歷、如何培養了自己的專業能力和領域技能。

- 關於「教育背景」，你還能這樣説：

My degree in math gives me strong reasoning skills.
我讀的數學專業培養了我很強的邏輯思考能力。

My university provided me with a lot of networking opportunities.
我的大學提供了我很多建立人脈的機會。

I didn't pursue a Master's degree right away because I felt that I needed to get some work experience prior to embarking on further studies.
我沒有立刻去讀碩士，因為我覺得在繼續鑽研學業之前，我需要先累積一些工作經驗。

pursue 追求	Master's degree 碩士學位	work experience 工作經驗
right away 立刻	prior to... 在……之前	embark on 著手

4. I have two years of experience in language teaching.

我有兩年的語言教學經驗。

> experience 經驗

介紹完了教育背景，如果你有工作經驗的話，你必須更著重於相關工作經驗的介紹，因為在很多領域，實務經驗是遠比理論儲備更重要的。介紹工作經驗時，必須把握住以下幾個重點：曾服務的公司、曾擔任的職務、服務時長和所見所學等。

• 關於「工作經驗」，你還能這樣說：

I've been working in Intel as a field engineer for five years.
我已經在英特爾當駐廠工程師五年了。

I've worked in a variety of roles and companies, which I've learned a lot from.
我在許多不同的公司擔任過各種不同的職位，從中我學到了很多。

I was hired as a project manager at HCL. I've been there for the past two years.
我在 HCL 公司當項目經理，過去兩年來都在該公司服務。

field engineer 駐廠工程師	a variety of 各式各樣的	role 職位
hire 聘用	project 項目	manager 經理

5. I've always loved material engineering.

我一直以來都很喜歡材料工程。

> material 材料／engineering 工程

介紹完了教育背景和工作經歷後，我們可以接著表達一下自己對於專業領域的熱情。這部分我們盡量要保持和前面兩點的聯繫，語言不浮誇，態度要誠懇，並且盡量維持明確的論述基調，才不會流於誇大和空泛。

- 關於「工作熱情」，你還能這樣說：

Ever since I graduated from college, I've been passionate about interior design.
自從我大學畢業後，我就一直對室內設計懷抱熱情。

I knew I wanted to go into acting from day one.
我一開始就知道我想要走演戲這條路。

I really enjoy the process of writing articles and getting feedback from the community.
我非常喜歡寫文章和聽取讀者回饋的過程。

ever since 自從	graduate 畢業	passionate 熱情的
interior 室內的	design 設計	act 演戲
from day one 一開始	process 過程	article 文章
feedback 回饋	community 社群	

6. I have extremely strong team-working skills.
我團隊合作的能力非常好。

extremely 極度地／ team-working 團隊合作／ skill 技能

這部分可能包含在 Tell me about yourself. 的自我介紹裡，也可能是面試官單獨問的：Tell me about your strengths.「說說你的優點。」或 Tell me about your weaknesses.「說說你的缺點。」中。這部分我們要注意語言的明確性和正向性。比如，講述優點時，不要只說 I consider myself a team player.「我是個善於團隊合作的人。」而是需再加上一個明確的例子，如：Whenever there is a conflict between our teammates, I would usually be the one to help facilitate communication and get it resolved.「每當我們團隊出現爭執時，我通常都是那一個出來協助溝通並解決問題的人。」而講述缺點時，也不要只說 I am a poor public speaker.「我不擅長公眾演講。」而是接著說 I've spent a lot of time working on it and now I'm more comfortable addressing a smaller audience.「我花了很多時間改進自己，現在我對一小群人演講時已經可以比較自在了。」

- 關於「自己的優缺點」，你還能這樣說：

I pride myself in being patient and communicative.
耐心和溝通能力是我自己引以為傲的特質。

My biggest weakness is my inability to multitask.
我最大的缺點就是我無法同時多工。

I'm not very good at public speaking.
我不太擅長公眾演講。

pride 使驕傲	patient 耐心的	communicative 善於溝通的
weakness 弱項	inability 無能	multitask 同時多工
public speaking 公眾演講		

7. I'm particularly interested in the latest project your company has been working on. 我對你們公司在進行的最新的案子特別感興趣。

particularly 特別地／ interested 感興趣的／ latest 最新的／ project 項目／ work on 執行

當面試官問到：Why are you interested in our company?「你為什麼對我們公司感興趣？」或 What attracted you to our company?「是什麼吸引你來應聘我們公司的？」時，就是在看你是否對應聘公司有足夠的了解。這時，就是考驗你真功夫的時候了，可不是瞎掰的功夫喔！而是是否真的有事先詳讀過目標公司的單位簡介、經營項目、最新動態和企業文化等。記住！你說得越明確，越能展現給面試主管：你是有做功課的！不妨試試以下這幾個句型，自己變換、應用一下喔！

- 關於「對公司的了解」，你還能這樣說：

I spent some time on your website reading about the position and the company.
我花了點時間在你們的網站上讀了有關這個職位和這間公司的相關資訊。

What really caught my eye was the friendly work environment you have. That's something I really appreciate.

真正讓我印象深刻的是你們友善的工作環境，那是我很欣賞的點。

I was impressed with the continuing education program you provide your employees.

我覺得貴公司提供給員工的繼續教育課程真的很棒。

spend 花費	website 網站	position 職位
appreciate 欣賞	friendly 友善的	environment 環境
catch one's eye 吸引到某人的注意	impress 使印象深刻	continuing education 繼續教育
program 課程	provide 提供	employee 員工

8. The reason why I left my previous job is that I'm looking for more professional growth and better career prospects.

我離開上一間公司的原因是我想尋找更多的專業提升和更好的職涯展望。

previous 先前的／ professional 專業的／ growth 成長／ career 職涯／ prospect 展望

當面試官問到：Why did you leave your last job?「你為什麼離開上一個崗位？」時，他們是想知道你對於工作的要求和你的長期職涯規劃是怎樣的。回答這題的原則是誠實、專業取向、不訴諸情緒。比如，千萬別說：I left my previous job because my former colleagues sucked!「我離開我上一份工作，因為我前同事爛透了！」

• 關於「離職原因」，你還能這樣說：

After many years of working in the office, I felt that I needed a new change.

在坐了那麼多年的辦公室後，我覺得我需要一次新的改變。

I felt that I had run out of room to grow professionally with JIS.

我覺得在 JIS 時在專業上已經沒有太多的成長空間。

I was laid off from my previous position due to company downsizing.
因為公司進行機構精簡，所以我被遣散了。

run out of 耗盡	room 空間	professionally 專業上
lay off 遣散	previous 先前的	due to 由於
downsizing 裁員		

9. I'm looking forward to putting my well-honed expertise to work. 我期待將我精熟的專業應用到工作上。

look forward to 期待／ put...to work 應用／ well-honed 精熟的／ expertise 專業能力

當面試官問到：Where do you see yourself in X years?「你的 X 年工作規劃是什麼？」時，他們是想知道你的短、中、長期職涯規劃，以及目標公司可以為你帶來什麼專業上的獲得。此時，你也可以依照自己的短、中、長期職涯規劃來組織自己的回答。

• 關於「未來展望」，你還能這樣說：

In three years, I would like to be in an upper management position.
三年後，我希望可以擔任高階管理職務。

I plan on being ready for a bigger role and more responsibilities.
我計畫讓自己可以承擔更大的職位和更多的責任。

I'm very open to whatever opportunities the future may hold.
我對於未來的任何機會都非常歡迎。

upper 高階的	management 管理	position 職位
role 職位	responsibility 責任	open 歡迎的
whatever 任何的	opportunity 機會	hold 握有

10. Can you tell me a little about the team that I will be working with? 你可以稍微跟我說一下要和我共事的這個團隊的情況嗎？

team 團隊

最後，當面試官問到：Do you have any questions for me about the company? 「你對於這間公司有什麼問題想問嗎？」時，這是一個很好的機會讓你能針對你想深入了解的問題發問。雖然這是一個是非問題，但如果你回答 Not really!「沒有欸！」會顯得你對這份工作一點好奇都沒有，這樣還是會讓面試官多少對你打折扣的。因此，我們最後來學學有哪些可以向面試主管提問的問題吧！

- 關於「向公司發問」，你還能這樣說：

What does a typical day look like?
在這裡一般的工作日大致是怎麼樣的情形？

What's your favorite part about working here?
你在這裡工作最喜歡的點是什麼？

Will there be opportunities for professional training and advancement?
這邊會有專業訓練和專業發展的機會嗎？

typical 典型的	training 訓練	advancement 發展

 跟面試有關的慣用語

1. dead end job 毫無前途的工作

哈哈：I'm feeling stuck in a dead end job.
我感覺我被困在一個毫無前途的工作。

Lyla：At least you have a job.
至少你還有工作。

2. an iron will　鐵一般的意志

哈哈：My friends always say I have an iron will.
　　　我朋友都說我有鐵一般的意志。

Lyla：While you're sleeping?
　　　當你在睡覺的時候？

3. the eleventh hour　最後一刻

哈哈：I got his email at the eleventh hour telling me the interview was cancelled.
　　　我到最後一刻才收到他的電郵，告訴我這次的面試取消了。

Lyla：What? After so much effort you put in?
　　　什麼？你都準備這麼久了！

4. a bird's eye view　概觀

哈哈：Did you discuss money?
　　　你們有討論到薪水嗎？

Lyla：Yeah! He did give me a bird's eye view of the compensation package.
　　　有！他給我概括看了一下薪資福利的條件。

5. hand in hand　關係密切

哈哈：I wish I could be as confident as Jerry.
　　　我希望我可以有像 Jerry 一樣的自信。

Lyla：Confidence goes hand in hand with experience.
　　　自信和經驗是密不可分的。

第 11 章　哈啦工作

角色：哈哈（來自台灣）、Lyla（來自美國）

工作是一個很好聊的話題，不管你是在找工作、想換工作、介紹自己的工作或抱怨工作，工作都是一個安全且很好開展的話題。現在，就讓我們一起來學找工作、跳槽、爽缺和吐槽上司用英文怎麼說吧！

1. I am currently working for a travel agency based in Osaka.
我現在在大阪的一間旅行社上班。

> currently 目前／ work for 在……工作／ travel agency 旅行社／ based 以……為基地／ Osaka 大阪

介紹自己的職業時，可以用以下句型：I'm a ＋職業、I work for ＋公司、I work in ＋領域、I work as ＋職業。如果要進一步介紹該公司，可以說：It's a company that… 比如：It's a company that manages publicity for other companies.「它是一間幫其他公司管理公關事務的公司。」

• 關於「介紹職業」，你還能這樣說：

I work in online education.
我做線上教育的。

I'm working as a kindergarten teacher in Taipei.
我現在在台北當幼兒園老師。

I'm a software engineer.
我是一位軟體工程師。

online education 線上教育	software 軟體	engineer 工程師

2. I'm responsible for recruiting. 我負責招聘。

responsible 負責的／ recruit 招聘

介紹自己在公司裡負責什麼，我們可以說：I'm responsible for...「我負責……。」
比如：I'm responsible for managing a sales team.「我負責管理一個銷售團隊。」
而「管理」我們可以用：supervise、oversee、run 或 manage 等動詞。

- 關於「工作項目」，你還能這樣說：

I manage the local engineering team.
我管理當地的工程團隊。

I run the IT department.
我負責 IT 部門。

I look after our clients in the Asia-Pacific region.
我負責亞太地區的客戶。

manage 管理	local 當地的	engineering 工程的
team 團隊	run 經營管理	IT 資訊技術
department 部門	look after 照顧	client 客戶
Asia-Pacific 亞太	region 地區	

3. I'm self-employed. 我自己創業。

self-employed 自己創業的

employ 意思是「雇用」，因此，self-employed 顧名思義就是「自己雇用自
己」，也就是自己當老闆的意思啦！而有所不同的是 freelancer「自由業者」，
freelancer 可能是自己跟不同的公司簽約、接案子，並自主在家完成，而 self-
employed 則是指自己開公司、當老闆，並且純粹做自己的公司或事業的人。

- 關於「自己創業」，你還能這樣說：

I run my own business.
我自己開公司。

I work for myself.

我自己當老闆。

I'm a business owner.

我自己當老闆。

run 經營	busines 事業	owner 擁有者

4. I'm between jobs at the moment.　　我現在還在找工作。

between jobs 找工作中

「沒工作」最簡單直接的說法就是 jobless 或 unemployed。如果要委婉一點的話，我們可以說：between jobs，「在工作和工作之間的空擋」也就相當於沒有工作啦！而關於「結束工作」還分為幾種不同的情況，如：resign「辭職」是指自己提出辭呈而辭職；retire「退休」是指到了一定年紀而停止工作；fire 或 sack「解聘」是因工作表現或員工個人的因素而被免職；而 lay off「遣散」則是因人事成本或公司本身的因素而被遣散。

• 關於「沒工作」，你還能這樣說：

I'm not working at the moment.

我現在沒工作。

I've been unemployed for almost three years.

我已經快三年沒工作了。

I'm retired.

我退休了。

unemployed 失業的	retired 退休的

5. It's easy money. I don't have anything to complain about.

這份工作滿輕鬆的，我沒什麼好抱怨的。

> easy money 輕鬆的工作／ complain 抱怨

當別人問到你：How do you like your job?「你覺得你的工作怎麼樣？」你可以像以下這樣來回答：It's stress-free. I enjoy it.「沒什麼壓力，我滿喜歡的。」、It's easy money, to be honest.「滿輕鬆的老實講。」、I can work from the comfort of my home.「我可以在我家舒適的環境工作。」、I'm just a typical 9-to-5er. Nothing special.「我只是個朝九晚五的普通上班族，沒什麼特別的。」

- 關於「描述工作」，你還能這樣說：

You have a cushy job.
你的工作好爽喔！

It's just a regular 9-to-5 job.
這只是一個普通的朝九晚五的工作。

It's a job that involves a lot of traveling.
這是一份需要很常出差的工作。

cushy 輕鬆的	regular 普通的	involve 包含

6. How's the pay?　薪水怎麼樣？

> pay 薪水

談到薪水就稍微比較敏感了，切記只限好友之間才比較好聊薪水喔！問對方「薪水如何？」我們可以這樣問：How's the pay? 或 Do they pay you well?「你薪水好嗎？」回答時，通常會說：The pay is alright.「薪水還行。」

- 關於「薪水」，你還能這樣說：

Is it good money?
薪水好嗎？

They pay me a lot more than my last job.
我現在的薪水比我之前的工作好多了。

I was well-paid and I enjoyed my job.
我當時薪水不錯，而且我很喜歡我的工作。

> **well-paid** 薪水高的

7. He's a nice guy and he can play hardball when he has to.

他人很好，但他強硬起來時也是很強硬的。

> play hardball 強硬

上司，就是我們常說的 boss，可能是你工作上最大的夢魘，有時候也可能成為你一輩子的貴人，總之，人生中要遇到一位好上司確實很難啊！關於好上司、壞上司，我們來學學英文怎麼說。

• 關於「上司」，你還能這樣說：

Why does he always find fault with everything I do?
為什麼他老是找我麻煩？

He doesn't know what he's doing.
他根本不會辦事。

He has no airs and graces. Very approachable.
他沒有架子，非常好親近。

find fault with 找麻煩	**have no airs and graces** 沒有架子
approachable 易親近的	

8. I'm in the middle of a pile of work. 我還有一大堆工作要做。

> in the middle of 在……之中／ pile 堆

in the middle of... 「正在……」在英文中是非常常見的表達法，比如：in the middle of nowhere「所在地非常偏僻」、in the middle of a meeting「正在開會」等。因此，如果要說「你現在有事嗎？」我們可以說：In the middle of something? 而如果要說「我的行程很滿。」我們可以說：I have a tight schedule.、I'm on a tight schedule. 或 I'm working to a tight agenda.。

- 關於「工作忙碌」，你還能這樣說：

It's been a crazy week.

這個禮拜好忙啊！

Thursday always feels like the longest day of the week.

星期四老是感覺像一星期中最長的一天。

I have a heavy workload.

我的工作量很大。

---

workload 工作量

---

9. I am looking for a new job. 我在找新工作。

look for 尋找

look for a job 是「找工作」；find a job、land a job、get a job 是「找到工作」；而「找工作」這個過程可以叫 job hunting；而「找工作的人」我們可以説是 job seeker。

- 關於「找工作」，你還能這樣說：

It's really difficult to land a job in the US at this moment.

現在在美國找工作很難。

I'm trying to find a job in finance.

我在找金融相關的工作。

I got the job!

我錄取了！

---

land a job 找到工作 | **finance** 金融

---

10. I heard more people are looking to jump ship to the new school.　我聽說有更多人想要跳槽到那間新學校。

> look to 打算／ jump ship 跳槽

最後，我們來學學「跳槽」、「挖角」、「獵人頭」在英文中怎麼表達。首先，「跳槽」我們會說 jump ship「跳船」；而「挖角」我們則可以用 poach 或 headhunt。poach 原本是指「非法捕獵」，這邊則引伸為「挖角」。

- 關於「跳槽」，你還能這樣說：

She tried to headhunt him but that fell through.
她想要挖角他，但最後失敗了。

A former employee has been poaching our staff lately.
一位前任員工最近一直挖角我們的職員。

He's a job hopper.
他經常換工作。

headhunt 挖角	fall through 失敗	former 前任的
employee 員工	poach 挖角	staff 員工
lately 最近	job hopper 經常換工作的人	

 跟工作有關的慣用語

1. have a lot on my plate　事情很多

哈哈：You said you would call me back.
　　　妳說妳會回電給我的。

Lyla：Sorry, I forgot. I had a lot on my place then.
　　　抱歉，我忘記了，我當時事情很多。

2. bread and butter　吃飯的傢伙

哈哈：Well done, Lyla! I didn't know you were this good at singing.
　　　唱得不錯欸！ Lyla ！我以前都不知道妳歌唱得這麼棒。

Lyla：That's my bread and butter now!
　　　那是我現在吃飯的傢伙啊！

3. moonlight　兼職

Lyla：Why do you always look so tired?
　　　你為什麼每次都看起來這麼累？

哈哈：I don't sleep well. I moonlight as a bartender after work.
　　　我睡不好，我下班之後還要去兼職當調酒師。

4. on the back burner　不太重要

哈哈：How's your singing career going so far?
　　　妳的歌唱事業最近怎麼樣啊？

Lyla：Not much! Actually that's already on the back burner.
　　　沒怎樣！其實我早就不太唱歌了。

5. throw in the towel　放棄

哈哈：Need some help with your work?
　　　工作需要幫忙嗎？

Lyla：It's fine. I'm about to throw in the towel.
　　　沒關係，我都快放棄了。

第 12 章　哈啦金錢

角色：哈哈（來自台灣）、Lyla（來自美國）

俗話説：談錢傷感情，但有時候不把錢談妥更傷感情！人與人之間多少會有金錢往來，即便沒有，兩人金錢觀的異同還是可能會影響交際中的各種大小事。現在，就讓我們一起來庸俗地哈啦金錢吧！

1. They're filthy rich. 他們超有錢的！

> filthy 骯髒的

要表達「某人超有錢」，除了説：They're rich.「他們很有錢。」之外，我們也很常聽到：They're filthy rich.「他們超級有錢！」其中，filthy rich 帶有一點嫉富的心態，有點「有錢到很討厭」的感覺，也可以説成 stinking rich。另外，loaded 也可以用來表示「有錢」，字面上可以理解成「裝滿了錢」的意思。

• 關於「有錢」，你還能這樣說：

Money is no object.
錢不是問題。

He has money to burn.
他錢多得花不完。

They don't really have to work. They're loaded.
他們不怎麼需要工作，他們有錢得很。

object 事物	loaded 有錢的

2. I wish I was born with a silver spoon in my mouth.
我真希望我是個富二代。

> silver 銀的

「富二代」不能説成 second rich generation。最常見的説法是：be born with a silver spoon in one's mouth「含著銀湯匙出生」或 trust fund baby「富二代」。其他的説法還有：He's from a well-off family.「他來自一個富裕家庭。」或 He's from a family of means.「他的家境優渥。」

- 關於「富二代」，你還能這樣說：

That guy is a trust fund baby.

那傢伙是個富二代。

Her husband actually comes from money.

她老公其實家境很好的。

She's from a relatively well-to-do family.

她來自一個相對富裕的家庭。

trust fund baby 富二代	relatively 相對地	well-to-do 富裕的

3. I'm a little light on funds until the tenth.　　我到十號之前都有點吃緊。

light on funds　手頭吃緊

朋友找你唱歌、吃大餐時，如果剛好遇到自己手頭吃緊，我們有以下幾種說法：light on funds、short on cash、low on cash、tight on money、strapped for cash 等。比如：I'm running low on cash. I'll take a rain check. 「我現在手頭有點吃緊，這次先不去了。」另外，中文的「吃老本」在英文中也有類似的說法：eat into savings。

- 關於「手頭吃緊」，你還能這樣說：

I'm strapped for cash.

我手頭有點吃緊。

I'm too hard up for cash.

我最近有點窮。

So you're just eating into your savings?

所以你就這樣一直吃老本嗎？

strapped for cash 手頭吃緊	hard up 手頭吃緊	savings 存款

4. He owes a lot of money.　他欠了很多錢。

> **owe 欠**

「借錢」最簡單的說法就是 borrow money from…，如：I'd like to borrow one hundred dollars until the 20th.「我想跟你借一百元，二十號還你。」相反地，「借別人錢」則是 lend，如：I'm lending you two hundred .「我先借你兩百。」而「還錢」則是 pay you back，如：Let me borrow 1,800. I will pay you back on payday.「借我一千八，我發薪日會還你。」向別人借錢後，自己便會處於 in debt「負債」的狀態，而「還清」債務的英文則是 pay off the debt。

- 關於「借錢」，你還能這樣說：

I am in debt.
我現在負債。

He'll have to declare bankruptcy.
他必須申請破產。

How could you lend her so much money?
你怎麼可以借她那麼多錢？

in debt 負債	declare 宣布	bankruptcy 破產
lend 借出		

5. She has to work three different jobs to scrape by.
她必須打三份工才能勉強度日。

> **scrape by 勉強過日子**

scrape by 字面上的意思是「擠身而過」，在這裡是指「勉強糊口」。同樣的意思也可以用 struggle「艱難度日」這個詞，如：I'm struggling a little.「我現在日子過得有點艱難。」

- 關於「經濟拮据」，你還能這樣說：

I was flat broke.
我當時完全沒有錢。

I was down and out.
我當時窮困潦倒。

I was so badly off that I couldn't even afford my rent.
我當時窮到連房租都付不起。

flat broke 破產的	down and out 窮困潦倒	badly off 窮困
afford 付得起	rent 房租	

6. He's living from paycheck to paycheck.　他是個月光族。

live from paycheck to paycheck　月光族

所謂的「月光族」，也就是每個月把錢花光光的人，在英文中，我們可以用 live from paycheck to paycheck 這個說法，字面上是說：在每個月的工資之間生存。而我們常說的「花錢如流水」，在英文中竟然也有對應的句子：spend money like water，是不是很神奇呢！

- 關於「花錢如流水」，你還能這樣說：

How long do you think you can spend money like water?
你覺得你可以再像這樣花錢如流水多久？

I really enjoy splashing out from time to time.
我挺喜歡這樣偶爾毫無顧忌地揮霍的。

Money burns a hole in my pocket. I always end up spending more than I realize.
我總是花錢如流水，花出去那麼多錢自己都不曉得。

splash out 揮霍	burn 燒	hole 洞
realize 知曉		

7. She's such a cheapskate.　她超小氣的。

> cheapskate　吝嗇的人

「小氣鬼，喝涼水」，在英文中，「小氣」的說法也相當多喔！除了 stingy「小氣的」之外，tight-fisted、cheapskate、tightwad、scrooge 和 penny-pincher 都可以用來形容小氣的人。

• 關於「小氣」，你還能這樣說：

He's a tightwad.
他真是個小氣鬼。

She's a real scrooge.
她真是個吝嗇鬼。

I'm tired of my penny-pinching father.
我受夠了我那小氣的老爸。

tightwad　小氣鬼	scrooge　吝嗇鬼	penny-pinching 吝嗇的

8. I'm pretty careful with my money.　我花錢滿謹慎的。

> careful　謹慎的

「小氣」和「節儉」往往是一線之隔，可是褒貶的語氣卻天差地遠。但兩者在許多行為上還是有很多雷同點的，比如一個 stingy「小氣」的人肯定是會 be very careful with money「花錢謹慎」，或有 save money 或 put aside some money「存點錢」的習慣。而「節儉」在英文中有兩個常見的形容詞：frugal 和 thrifty。其中，frugal 是指「不願意花錢的人」，而 thrifty 則是形容「經濟、不浪費的人」，兩者還是有細微的差別。

• 關於「節儉」，你還能這樣說：

She's a frugal person.
她是一個節儉的人。

I understand you want to save some cash.
我理解你想要省點錢。

You need to cut back on your spending.
你需要減少你的支出。

frugal 節儉的	cash 現金	cut back on 縮減
spending 花費		

9. The price of everything has gone through the roof.　物價飆漲。

price 價格／go through the roof 飆漲

現在這個時代就是什麼都漲，就剩薪水沒漲。其中，「物價」的英文是 price of goods，而「物價上漲」我們可以說：The price of goods is rising.，或用 has gone through the roof 衝破屋頂似的「飆漲」。另外，我們也可以說：Prices are biting hard at my wallet.「物價好高，我的荷包失血。」

• 關於「物價」，你還能這樣說：

Everything is so high right now.
現在什麼東西都好貴！

I heard Bristol is expensive.
我聽說在布里斯托生活很昂貴。

Prices are biting.
物價好高啊！

bite 咬人

10. How are you gonna afford your food, gas, rent and everything? 你要怎麼負擔你的吃飯、汽油、房租那一大堆東西？

afford 付得起／ rent 房租

許多人嚮往早日經濟獨立，但真正經濟獨立後，所有的經濟責任都必須自己一肩扛下了。想必以下這些句子都不陌生吧！如：How are you gonna afford your food, gas, rent and everything?「你要怎麼負擔你的吃飯、汽油、房租那一大堆東西？」其中，…and everything 就是中文裡面常說的「之類的」的意思。

- 關於「經濟責任」，你還能這樣說：

I can't just walk away from my financial obligations.
我不能就這樣丟下我的經濟責任不管啊！

After going back, I still need to get my student loans sorted out.
我回去之後還要想辦法還我的學貸。

He's three months behind on his mortgage payments.
他已經三個月沒付房貸了。

financial 財務的	obligation 義務	student loan 學貸
sort out 解決	behind 落後	mortgage payment 房貸

 跟金錢有關的慣用語

1. bread and butter 吃飯的傢伙

哈哈：I didn't you are this good at drawing comics.
　　　我不知道妳這麼會畫漫畫。

Lyla：Of course! That's my bread and butter.
　　　當然囉！那是我吃飯的傢伙。

2. live from hand to mouth　勉強糊口

哈哈：Her father earns very little. They're living from hand to mouth.
她爸爸賺得錢很少，他們只能勉強糊口度日。

Lyla：I feel so bad for them. Let's give them some help!
好可憐啊！我們幫他們一下吧！

3. make ends meet　勉強維持生計

哈哈：I kinda find it hard to make ends meet living in a big city.
我覺得在大城市生活好難維持生計啊！

Lyla：Yeah! It's always how much you've got left at the end of the month that matters.
對啊！其實你要看你到月底的時候存下了多少錢比較重要。

4. marry money　為了錢結婚

哈哈：Whether you agree or not, marry money!
不管妳同不同意，嫁個有錢人吧！

Lyla：I can't believe I'm agreeing with you! It's an ugly fact, but so damn true.
我真不敢相信我竟然同意你的說法，很殘酷卻很真實！

5. self-made man　白手起家的人

哈哈：Unlike those spoiled millennials, he's every inch a self-made man!
不像那些被寵壞的千禧寶寶，他完全是靠自己白手起家的。

Lyla：True! He's so admirable.
就是啊！他超厲害的。

第 13 章　哈啦股票

角色：哈哈（來自台灣）、Lyla（來自美國）

如果你老是覺得無法真正融入老外的朋友圈，除了基本的溝通能力外，你可能還需要考慮一下是不是自己在特定領域的常識和相關語言能力的不足所造成的。人嘛！在社會上什麼東西都知道一點總是比較好交流。比如當朋友們在大聊股票時，如果自己對於股票的常識是零，連一句話都插不上，別人就再也不會找你聊這個話題了。本章節，就讓我們一起來粗淺地哈啦股票吧！

1. Mark owns 25% of the company.

Mark 有這間公司百分之二十五的所有權。

> own 擁有

當要和別人說：「我有⋯⋯公司的股票。」時，我們可以說：I have ／ own ／ hold shares in this company.。其中，share 指的就是「股份」或「股票」。或更簡單地說：I'm invested in this company.「我投資了這間公司。」

• 關於「擁有股票」，你還能這樣說：

I hold 500 dollars worth of shares in BTS.
我在 BTS 公司有五百元等值的股票。

I have 2,000 shares in this company.
我有這間公司的兩千張股票。

I am invested in Apple.
我投資了蘋果公司。

hold 持有	worth 價值	share 股份
invest 投資		

2. TTW is worth $56.08 per share.

TTW 公司每股價值 56.08 美元。

> worth 價值／ per 每

要表達「某公司每股價值多少」，我們可以說：...is worth...dollars per share。當中的 worth 作為形容詞，後面直接加數字。另外，如果要說「公司市值」，我們可以用 market capitalization 或 market value。

- 關於「股價」，你還能這樣說：

TRPC has a market capitalization of 350 billion dollars.
TRPC 公司目前市值三千五百億美元。

Central Jakarta has a book value of $45.2 per share.
Central Jakarta 目前每股帳面價值為 45.2 美元。

TASCO was traded at a record high of 900 dollars one month ago.
TASCO 一個月前的交易價格創下九百美元的歷史新高。

market capitalization 市值	billion 十億	book value 帳面價值
trade 交易	record high 歷史新高	

3. Tesla went public in June 2010 at a price of 17 dollars per share. 特斯拉在 2010 年六月以每股十七美元的價格上市。

> go public 上市／ price 價格

關於「上市」，也就是公司開始於證券交易所公開交易股票的過程，我們有以下幾種說法：go public、start trading、float、launch its IPO（Initial Public Offering）。接著，我們就來看看這幾個詞是如何在句子中使用的。

- 關於「上市」，你還能這樣說：

The company will start trading March 4th.
這間公司三月四日開始銷售股份。

He floated his company in the stock market.
他上市了他的公司。

FQ Logistics officially launched its IPO last month.
FQ 物流上個月正式首次公開募股。

trade 交易	float 使上市	logistics 物流
officially 正式地	launch 發佈	IPO（Initial Public Offering） 首次公開募股

4. The Dow Jones is up 400 points. 道瓊工業指數上漲四百點。

> Dow Jones 道瓊工業指數／ up 上升

關於「股票上漲」的表達法很多。如果你有聽財經新聞的習慣，你可能常聽到 skyrocket「飆升」、jump「躍升」、rise「上升」、climb「攀升」、take off「飆漲」、gain「獲得」等。如果要說「上升……點」，可以直接在動詞後加數字，如：Dow Jones rose ／ gained 200 points.「道瓊指數上升了兩百點。」；如果要說：「上升到……」，則需要加 to，如：S & P 500 climbed to all-time highs.「S & P 500 指數攀升到歷史新高點。」另外，更簡單的說法是以 up 當形容詞用：Dow Jones was up 400 points.「道瓊指數上漲四百點。」

• 關於「股票上漲（一）」，你還能這樣說：

The Dow Jones surged to a record high on Wednesday.
道瓊指數於星期三攻上歷史新高點。

The Dow Jones was up over 300 points late-morning Monday at 30905..
道瓊指數週一上午上揚超過三百點來到 30905 點。

The Nasdaq opened at a record high on Tuesday.
那斯達克指數週二開盤創新高。

surge 狂飆	record high 歷史新高	Nasdaq 那斯達克指數
open 開盤		

5. S & P rallies 570 points.　S & P 指數反彈 570 點。

> rally　重新振作

除了上述的「上漲」說法外，我們還可以用其他更形象的表達。如：rally 可表示「重新振作」、「谷底反彈」。on fire 表示「發威」、「勢頭正熱」。另外，pullback 也可以表示「反彈」、「回升」。多聽、多看財經新聞，我們都可以學到更多新穎的表達詞彙喔！

• 關於「股票上漲（二）」，你還能這樣說：

Solar Energy Stocks are on fire today.
太陽能股今天發威了。

Nasdaq is trading higher.
那斯達克指數走高。

There's a pullback in clean-tech stocks.
綠能科技股出現反彈。

solar energy　太陽能	on fire　發威	pullback　拉回
clean-tech　綠能科技		

6. The Nasdaq ended lower.　那斯達克收盤時下跌。

> end　收盤

關於「開盤」和「收盤」我們可以直接說：open 和 end。如果「開盤走高」，我們可以說：open higher；而「收盤下跌」則是 end lower，反之亦然。而股票下跌當然也有非常多動詞可以表示，如：down「下跌」、fall「下跌」、tumble「崩盤」、plummet「重挫」、plunge「下竄」、collapse「崩盤」、take a dive「暴跌」、take a nosedive「暴跌」、lose ground「失守」等。和 up 一樣，down 也可以同時作為動詞和形容詞用。

• 關於「股票下跌（一）」，你還能這樣說：

The Dow tumbled more than 10.5%.
道瓊指數重挫超過百分之十點五。

The Stoxx Europe 600 Index slumped 2.3 per cent.

泛歐 600 指數下滑二點三個百分點。

Facebook's shares plunged below the $600 mark.

臉書股價跌破六百美元大關。

tumble 重挫	index 指數	slump 下滑
plunge 下竄	mark 標誌	

7. Stocks are in the red. 股票都下跌了。

in the red 出現赤字

與華人文化中紅色代表吉利的觀念相反，red 在財政上是「赤字」、「虧損」的意思。相反地，black 則是指「盈餘」。因此，「下跌」我們還可以說：in the red；而「上漲」則是 in the black.。

• 關於「股票下跌（二）」，你還能這樣說：

Dow sheds 600 points in a day.

道瓊指數一天之內掉了六百點。

Stocks got hammered again today.

股市今天又崩盤了。

Tech stocks took a hammering today.

科技股今天崩盤了。

shed 脫落	hammer 重擊	take a hammering 重挫

8. Asian stocks are mixed today.　亞洲股今天漲跌互見。

> mixed　好壞參半的

當然，股票不可能都是一路長紅或一路低迷，尤其隨著時局的變動、消息的釋出，漲跌起伏的情形更是常見。而「有漲有跌」的英文我們可以用 mixed 這個詞。mixed 的原意是「混合的」，也可以理解成「好壞參半的」。比如：I have mixed feelings about him.「我對他的情感好壞參半。」另外，「漲跌起伏」我們還可以用 fluctuating「起伏」和 volatile「易波動的」來表示。

- 關於「股票起伏」，你還能這樣說：

With the pandemic, it's always fluctuating.
因為疫情，股票市場都起起伏伏。

World stocks have been on a roller coaster ride in the first half of 2020.
全球股市在 2020 的前半年一直像在坐雲霄飛車。

The stock market is so volatile today.
最近的股市好波動。

pandemic　疫情	fluctuate　波動	roller coaster　雲霄飛車
ride　搭乘	volatile　波動的	

9. The time of the bull market is over.　牛市已經過去了。

> bull market　牛市

bull market「牛市」是指向上的市場趨勢，而 bear market「熊市」則是往下的市場趨勢。可以這樣想像：牛角往「上」長，而熊爪向「下」扒。其他的術語還有：blue chip stock「藍籌股」，又稱「績優股」，是指大型而穩健的公司股票。limit up 是「漲停板」，而 limit down 是「跌停板」。crash 和 meltdown 則是指「股災」。

- 關於「股票術語」，你還能這樣說：

It's considered a blue chip stock.
它被認為是一支藍籌股。

He calls it the biggest crash ever.
他稱這次是史上最嚴重的一次股災。

BOJ shares hit limit up.
BOJ 股票漲停板。

| consider 認為 | blue chip stock 藍籌股 | crash 股災 |
| hit 達到 | limit up 漲停板 | |

10. You want to be very careful in stock picking.
你在選擇股票時要非常小心。

> pick 選擇

各種投資都有賺有賠，最後不免俗地來幾句常見的投資建議吧！ You want to be very careful in stock picking. 「你在選擇股票時要非常小心。」其中，you want to… 不需要理解成「你想要……」，而是「你最好……」或「你應該……」；相反地，you don't want to… 也不是「你不想要……」，而是「你最好不要……」的意思。

- 關於「投資建議」，你還能這樣說：

Set the goal and stay the course.
設立目標，堅定方向。

There's too much at stake to put it all on the line for a single stock.
把所有資金都投在一支股票上風險太大了。

Diversifying your portfolio protects you from the ups and downs of the stock market.
將你的投資組合多樣化可以降低股市波動的影響。

set 設立	goal 目標	course 路線
at stake 有風險	on the line 處於危險中	single 單一的
diversify 多樣化	portfolio 投資組合	ups and downs 漲跌
stock market 股市		

1. laughing stock 笑柄

哈哈：Look at my hair. It's so messed up. I'm gonna be the laughing stock of the school.
看看我的頭髮，整個剪壞了！我要成為整個學校的笑柄了。

Lyla：Don't worry. You already are.
別擔心！你已經是了啊！

2. play the stock market 玩股票

哈哈：I made 35,000 dollars playing the stock market this summer.
我這個夏天玩股票賺進了三萬五美金。

Lyla：Wow! I didn't know you understand the stock market.
哇！我不知道你也懂股票耶！

3. play with fire 玩火（做冒險的事）

哈哈：I think I'm gonna put in another 10,000 dollars.
我覺得我會再投入十萬美元吧！

Lyla：You can't be serious! You're playing with fire!
你在開玩笑吧！你這是在玩火啊！

4. blow it all on... 把錢都砸在……上

哈哈：I am kinda low on funds now cause I blew it all on the stocks.
我現在手邊沒什麼錢，因為我都砸在股票上了。

Lyla：Are you nuts? You haven't even got your student loans sorted out!
你瘋了嗎？你的學貸都還沒付清欸！

5. My gut tells me... 我的直覺告訴我……

哈哈：You think it's a good timing to buy more?
妳覺得現在是繼續買進的好時機嗎？

Lyla：My gut tells me you need to take a beat.
我的直覺告訴我你應該緩一緩。

第14章　哈啦買房

角色：哈哈（來自台灣）、Lyla（來自美國）

人到了一定的年紀，難免要面對「買房」的問題，然而，這種「大件玩具」可不是像買菜一樣說買就買，說後悔就後悔的，而是需要經歷一段漫長的找房、看房、諮詢的過程。當然，對多數的普通人來說，還有籌款的問題。本章節著眼於常見的買房相關會話，讓不懂房地產的人也可以用英語輕鬆哈啦買房。

1. I'm currently looking at homes. 我最近在看房子。

> currently 最近／ look at 查看

買房子前的一個重要的前期作業當然就是找資料、做功課啦！在計畫買房的階段，除了衡量自己的經濟能力外，鎖定區域、確定房型、觀察周邊等功夫至少都會花上好幾個月甚至若干年的時間。而當你要和朋友分享自己最近在看房子、物色房子時，用英文我們可以這樣說：I'm currently looking at homes.「我最近在看房子。」其中，look at 有「仔細看」的意思，而「房子」我們說 house 或 home 都可以。另外一個好用的句型是 I'm looking to…「我最近計畫要……。」

• 關於「計畫買房」，你還能這樣說：

I've been browsing the market for at least a year.
我已經看房子看了至少一年了。

I'm considering buying a house.
我在考慮要買房子。

I've been looking to buy a house these days.
我最近一直想要買房子。

browse 瀏覽	market 市場	at least 至少
consider 考慮	look to 尋求做某事	these days 最近

2. I'm interested in your house. Can we arrange a viewing?

我有興趣看你的**房子**，我們可以安排個時間看房嗎？

> interested 感興趣的／ arrange 安排／ viewing 參觀

當我們看到有興趣的建案，不管是新房還是二手房，我們都可以和對方説：I'm interested in your house. Can we arrange a viewing?「我有興趣看你的房子，我們可以安排個時間看房嗎？」所謂的 viewing 就是「實地看房」、「賞屋」，另外一種説法是 home tour。

- 關於「看房」，你還能這樣說：

Can you give me a model home tour?
你可以帶我參觀一下樣品屋嗎？

I really want this house! It's hard to sit and wait.
我真的很想買這棟房子，我不想再坐等了。

Can I book a second viewing?
我可以預約第二次賞屋嗎？

model home 樣品屋	tour 參觀	book 預約

3. How long has the property been up for sale?　這棟房子開賣多久了？

> property 房地產／ up for 參與／ sale 銷售

網路上或許多看房老手都會分享許多關於和屋主或房仲約看房賞屋時該注意的 tips「訣竅」，包含提前到現場看房、白天晚上各看一次、晴天雨天各看一次、觀察周邊的環境、進出的屋主等，但今天我們更多地來聊聊在賞屋時必問的幾個重要問題，如：How long has the property been up for sale?「這棟房子開賣多久了？」、What are the neighbors like?「這裡附近的住戶怎麼樣？」、Is there any allocated parking?「這邊有指定的停車位嗎？」、How old is the apartment complex?「這個社區多久了？」等。其中，有一個常見的中翻英錯誤是：「房屋社區」不是 community，而是 apartment building 或 apartment complex。community 是指社會上的「社群」或「共同體」。

- 關於「買房前要問的重要問題」，你還能這樣說：

Is there room to negotiate the price?

有議價空間嗎？

How many offers have they had?

他們得到幾次出價了？

I hope you don't mind me asking: why are you moving?

希望你別介意我這樣問：你為什麼要搬走啊？

room 空間	negotiate 協議	offer 出價
mind 介意		

4. How many square feet is your apartment?

你的公寓有多少平方英尺？

> square feet 平方英尺

美國是用 square feet「平方英尺」，其他地方大部分用 square meters「平米」。而台灣用的「坪」一坪約為 3.3 平米，在英文中沒有對應的詞。問「房屋有多大」時，我們可以說：How many square meters is it? 或直接問 How big is it? 另一個關於房子本身很重要的問題是 Is it decorated?「有帶裝潢嗎？」如果是所謂的「毛胚屋」，則是 undecorated「無裝修的」。而「附家具」與否，則可分為 fully-furnished「附完整家具的」、semi-furnished「附部分家具的」和 unfurnished「無附家具的」。

- 關於「房屋本身」，你還能這樣說：

Is it furnished?

有附家具嗎？

I'm looking for a two-bedroom apartment.

我在找兩房的公寓。

Do I get a view from here?

這裡有什麼視野嗎？

furnish 附家具的	view 視野

5. This place just works for us.　這個地方很適合我們。

> work for 適合

大家都想找到自己的 dream house「夢想中的房子」。然而，房屋這種超貴重商品，除了靠理性過濾之外，有時也得靠緣分。如果幸運地找到自己鍾意的房子，我們可以說：It is perfect for us.「這間對我們來說簡直完美。」或 This is our forever home.「這是我們要住一輩子的房子。」如果你只是先買來作跳板，則可以說：For me, it's just a stepping stone home.「對我來說，它只是間跳板房。」

- 關於「房子的優點」，你還能這樣說：

It's a great location, close to downtown, and the neighbors have been really welcoming.

它的地點很棒，離市區很近，鄰居也很友善。

I really like the convenience of my new apartment.

我很喜歡我新公寓的便利性。

I'd like it to be my forever home, so I'd like it to be lighter and more spacious.

我想要把它當作我久住的家，所以我想要它再更明亮、寬敞一點。

location 位置	downtown 市區	neighbor 鄰居
welcoming 友善、熱情的	convenience 便利性	apartment 公寓
forever 永遠的	light 明亮的	spacious 寬敞的

6. It can get very noisy, even at night, because it's close to the main road.

這裡有時會很吵，即使到晚上的時候還是一樣，因為它離主要道路很近。

> main road 主要道路

關於房屋的缺點，比較普遍的不外乎噪音、採光、空氣不流通、寒氣、潮濕等問題。我們可以用 It can get…「它會……。」這個句型，如：It can get very humid during the winter.「這裡冬天的時候會變得很潮濕。」另外有一個詞是 high-maintenance「難照料的」，也就是需要花很多金錢、精力來保養、維護的，這也可以算是房屋的一個缺點，如：It's pretty nice, but it's just a little high-maintenance.「這裡其實都滿好的，但就是維護成本有點高。」

• 關於「房子的缺點」，你還能這樣說：

It doesn't get much natural light during the day.
它白天的時候不太能接收得到自然光。

That one was a bit too cramped and stuffy.
那間的空間有點太窄小、空氣也不流通。

It can get very drafty in the winter.
它冬天的時候風會灌進來。

natural light 自然光	cramped 狹小的	stuffy 悶的
drafty 通風好的；風會灌進來的		

7. I'm putting a percentage of my income away every month for a down payment.

我現在一個月會把一部份的收入存起來準備付頭期款。

> put away 挪出／ percentage 百分比／ income 收入／
> down payment 頭期款

來到了買房財務周轉的部分，首先，頭期款的英文叫 down payment，如：I've been saving up for the down payment.「我一直在存錢準備付頭期款。」而「房

屋貸款」則是 home mortgage 或是 home loan。「申請房貸」我們會說：apply for a home mortgage 或 get a home loan。

• 關於「頭期、貸款」，你還能這樣說：

I'm putting 20 percent down first.
我要先付百分之二十的頭期款。

My wife and I currently have a 30-year fixed rate mortgage.
我和我老婆現在是用三十年的固定利率貸款。

I'm trying to get a home loan with 20 percent down.
我付了百分之二十的頭期款，現在要申請房屋貸款。

put 付	home loan 房屋貸款	down 已付款

8. The prices of houses are only going up.　房價只會上漲。

price 價格

「房價」的英文是 house prices 或 housing prices。一般我們都期待能買低賣高，也就是希望自己房子的房價會漲，而「上漲」最簡單的說法是 go up 或 rise。而我們在新聞上也常聽到政府祭出措施要「抑制房價上漲」，這句話的英文則是 cap the rising of house prices。

• 關於「房價漲跌」，你還能這樣說：

It might take awhile for home prices to stop increasing.
房價上漲還要過一陣子才會趨緩。

Property prices in this area have been stagnant for the past two years.
這個區域的房價過去兩年來都處於停滯狀態。

The bubble will burst soon.
房地產泡沫很快就會破的。

awhile 一陣子	increase 上漲	stagnant 停滯的
bubble 泡沫	burst 破	

9. I don't like the salesperson. Too pushy!

我不喜歡那個銷售員，太咄咄逼人了！

> salesperson 銷售員／pushy 咄咄逼人的

好的 real estate agent「房仲」非常有可能成為我們人生中的貴人，畢竟買房可是第一級別的人生大事啊！現在許多傳統印象中的 aggressive agent「咄咄逼人的房仲」都已經過時了。相反地，現在的人多半都會比較信任具有 honest and transparent「誠實、透明」特質的房仲。

- 關於「房仲」，你還能這樣說：

I like my realtor. She always has my best interests at heart.
我滿喜歡我的房仲的，她總是會為我的利益著想。

Are you real estate savvy?
你很懂房地產嗎？

Be wary of their sales pitches.
小心他們的話術。

realtor 房仲	have one's interests at heart 為某人的利益著想	
real estate 房地產	savvy 精通的	wary 警惕的
sales pitches 話術		

10. You need to make sure you have your finances in order.

你必須確定你有足夠的經濟實力。

> finance 財物／in order 狀況良好

最後，還是建議各位買房前一定要多聽、多看、多問、多走走。不管你買房是為了投資或自住，這些事前的努力都不會白費的。以下是幾句常見的買房建議。你還可以在說之前加上一句 disclaimer「免責聲明」：I'm not a real estate expert.「我不是房地產專家。」

- 關於「買房建議」，你還能這樣說：

You don't want to put your financial well-being at risk.
你不能拿你的財物狀況來冒險。

You have no business buying a house unless you have two million bucks in the bank.
除非你銀行裡有兩百萬元，否則你沒有資格買房子。

Buying a house is a huge commitment. You should make sure you're in a position to own a house.
買房子的投注非常大，你應該先確定自己有能力可以負擔得起一棟房子。

financial 財務的	well-being 狀況	put...at risk 使……冒險
have no business 沒資格	unless 除非	buck 美元
huge 巨大的	commitment 承諾	in a position to 能夠
own 擁有		

 跟買房有關的慣用語

1. house poor 房奴

哈哈：Don't you fancy owning your own house?
　　　妳不想擁有屬於自己的房子嗎？

Lyla：Not really! I don't want to be house poor.
　　　還好欸！我不想當房奴。

2. get a foot on the housing ladder 先買到第一間房

哈哈：Have you heard? Dereck has bought his second house.
　　　妳聽說了嗎？Dereck 買了他的第二間房子。

Lyla：Good for him. I don't even have the money to get a foot on the housing ladder.
　　　真好！我連買第一間房的錢都沒有。

3. get on like a house on fire　一拍即合

哈哈：I was worried about you meeting my friends, but you guys got on like a house on fire last night.

我一開始還擔心妳和我的朋友見面會尷尬什麼的，結果你們昨晚聊得可嗨了！

Lyla：They're good guys! I had a good time talking with them.

他們人很好啊！我跟他們聊得很開心。

4. There's no place like home.　還是家裡好。

哈哈：Finally back to Taiwan. There's no place like home.

終於回到台灣了，還是家裡好。

Lyla：Rent due next week.

下個月要繳房租囉！

5. go round the houses　廢話一大堆

哈哈：Going to the meeting?

去開會嗎？

Lyla：Yeah! It's the worst time of the day. I can't stand him going round the houses for 20 minutes every time.

對啊！一天中最痛苦的就是這個時候了。我受不了他每次都要先廢話個二十分鐘。

第15章 哈啦男人

角色：哈哈（來自台灣）、Lyla（來自美國）

姐妹淘聚會時最愛大聊男人了，各種炫耀、花痴、吐槽，既是一種增強凝聚力的儀式，也是一項定期排毒療程。本章就來教妳如何和外國姊妹一同暢聊男人，相信面對共同的「敵人」時，所有的想法都是超越文化、不分國籍的吧！

1. He's so attractive looking. 他長得好迷人啊！

attractive looking 長相迷人的

形容男人很「帥」，我們可以用以下幾個詞：

handsome「帥的」、good-looking「好看的」、attractive-looking「長得迷人的」。另外，cute「可愛的」和 hot「性感的」也常用來形容男人的外表。比如，一群女生聚在一起背著經過的小鮮肉說：He's so cute.「他好可愛喔！」

• 關於「男人真好看」，你還能這樣說：

He's hot!
他好帥！

He's a charming guy.
他是一個很迷人的男生。

You're more good-looking than I am.
你長得比我好看。

hot 帥的；美麗的；性感的	charming 迷人的	good-looking 好看的

2. Act your age a little. 成熟點好不好。

act one's age 行為符合年齡

很多時候，男人都會被認為幼稚、不成熟，這個時候就會被別人說：You're acting like a child.「你的行為好像小孩子。」或 Act your age a little!「成熟點好不好！」其中，act your age 其實是「行為符合年齡」的意思，除了可以用在幼

稚的情況，也可以指一個人過於早熟，比如：Aaron works so hard. Sometimes I wish he could act his age and hang out with his friends a bit.「Aaron 好用功，有時候我希望他可以像其他同齡的孩子一樣和他的朋友出去玩一玩。」

- 關於「男人真幼稚」，你還能這樣說：

Come on! You're a big boy!

拜託！你都長那麼大了！

How old are you, five?

你是五歲小孩嗎？

You're like a child sometimes.

你有時候像個小孩。

big boy 大人

3. You're such a guy.　你真是很男人啊！

such 如此／ guy 男人

在外用餐時，一位年輕貌美的妹子走過，身旁的男伴像是開了 X 光眼似的將她從頭掃到尾，下巴都合不上了，這時，妳就可以搧一下他的腦袋說：You're such a guy.「你真是很男人啊！」這句話根據不同語境會產生不同的含義。又比如：吃下午茶時，男伴毫無情趣地將精緻可愛的網紅蛋糕一口嚥下，一臉傻憨憨的樣子：You're such a guy.「你這個直男！」基本上就是 You're a typical guy.「你真是個典型的男人。」的意思。

- 關於「男人本色」，你還能這樣說：

He's a pervert.

他是個變態。

He's very flirtatious.

他很會撩別人。

Would you?
這個你可以嗎？

pervert 變態	flirtatious 打情罵俏的

4. There's a masculine look that I'm attracted to.
我會被一種很男性的外表吸引。

masculine 男子氣概的

「男子氣概」的英文是 masculinity，形容詞則是 masculine「具男子氣概的」。因此，「行為很男人」就是 act masculine，「穿著很男人」是 dress masculine，「說話很男人」則是 speak masculine。另外，「很 man」的英文形容詞還有 manly、macho 等。

- 關於「男子氣概」，你還能這樣說：

He's so manly.
他好有男子氣概。

I was trying to play macho in front of her.
我那時候想在她面前裝一下男子氣概。

Man up!
像個男人一點！

manly 有男子氣概的	play 演	macho 有男子氣概的

5. Growing up as a gay man, I naturally acted feminine.
我從小就是個男同性戀，所以我的行為舉止自然都比較女性化。

gay 同性戀的／ act 行為／ feminine 女性化的

「女性化」或所謂的「娘」，在英文中我們可以說：feminine、fem、girly 等。另外一個詞是 androgynous「雌雄莫辨的」，如：He has androgynous voice.「他的聲音雌雄莫辨。」

- 關於「陰柔男」，你還能這樣說：

I get made fun of and put down for being girly.
我因為行為比較女性化而被嘲笑、被數落。

You're so fem.
你好娘！

He looks like a chick.
他看起來像個女生。

make fun of 嘲笑	put down 奚落	girly 女孩子氣的
fem 女性化的	chick 女生	

6. It's probably part of the control thing.　這可能有點跟控制慾有關吧！

probably 可能／ control 控制／ thing ……相關的東西

男尊女卑、男性優越感、控制欲，這些傾向我們都可以叫 male chauvinism「男性沙文主義」，而 male chauvinist pig「男性沙文主義的豬」則是用來形容這種人。如果有人跟你抱怨男朋友經常吃醋生氣，你就可以回：It's probably part of the control thing.「這可能有點跟控制欲有關吧！」其中，thing 在這裡是指「……相關的東西」，經常放在要描述的名詞後面。

- 關於「大男人」，你還能這樣說：

He is a male chauvinist pig.
他是一隻大男人主義的豬。

Andrew is such a control freak.
Andrew 真是一個控制狂。

That's pure sexism.
那完全是性別主義啊！

male chauvinist 大男人主義者	control freak 控制狂	pure 純粹的
sexism 性別主義		

7. He's a one-woman kinda man.　他是用情專一的男人。

one-woman kinda man　專情的男人

很多人認為優質男的第一條件必須是用情專一、不花心。「專情男」我們可以說 one-woman kinda man 或 faithful「忠誠的」。其他優質男的特質還有：honest「誠實的」、romantic「浪漫的」、thoughtful「體貼的」、supportive「支持的」、confident「自信的」等。

- 關於「優質男」，你還能這樣說：

I'm always faithful.
我一直都很專情。

He caters to me all the time.
他總是順著我。

He's got a good head on his shoulders.
他是有頭腦的人。

faithful　忠誠的	cater to　順應	all the time　總是
have a good head on one's shoulders　有想法		

8. Many people say he's a player.　很多人都說他是個玩咖。

player　情場玩家

英文裡有各式各樣關於「渣男」的詞彙，如：

cheater、player、jerk、two-timer、womanizer、scumbag、love rat、bastard 等。情場上難免跌跌撞撞，渣男依舊層出不窮。但只要堅持正確的道路，活出更好的自我，總有一天真愛會降臨的。

- 關於「渣男」，你還能這樣說：

He's a total jerk.
他是個不折不扣的渣男。

He's a love rat.
他是個劈腿男。

What a bastard he is!
他真是個混帳！

jerk 混帳	love rat 劈腿男	bastard 混蛋

9. Guys are intimidated by pushy girls.
男人通常會被太主動的女生嚇到。

intimidate 使驚嚇／pushy 強勢的

很多人對大部分的男人都存在很強烈的刻板印象，但事實上，很多男生並不如大家認知中的那樣覺得的。這邊列了幾條膚淺卻真實存在的男人心裡話，男生們，有被說中嗎？

• 關於「男人喜惡」，你還能這樣說：

I like natural beauty, so I prefer girls with no makeup.
我喜歡自然美，所以我比較喜歡不化妝的女生。

Men are turned off by drama.
男人對情緒化很感冒。

Men like you to take interest in their interests.
男人喜歡你對他們的興趣也感興趣。

natural 自然的	beauty 美麗	prefer 更喜歡
makeup 化妝	turn off 使喪失興致	drama 情緒化
take interest in... 對……感興趣		

10. Men should take the initiative when it comes to those things.

在那些事情上男人應該要主動一點。

> take the initiative 主動／ when it comes to 在……上

重男輕女的觀念，雖然早已過時，卻還確實地存在於社會上，很多人仍受其所苦。同樣地，許多對於男人的傳統思想也依然很普遍，如：男兒有淚不輕彈、男兒膝下有黃金、男人是一家之主等，而這些句子轉換成英文又該怎麼表達呢？

• 關於「男人應該要」，你還能這樣說：

I think a man should be the breadwinner of the family.
我覺得男人應該要是一個家庭的主要經濟來源。

It would totally freak me out if I saw a man wearing makeup.
如果我看到男生化妝，我一定會嚇壞。

Be a man! Take responsibility for what you do.
像個男人一樣，為自己的行為負責。

| makeup 化妝 | totally 一定 | freak out 嚇壞 |
| breadwinner 主要經濟來源 | | take responsibility 負責 |

 跟男人有關的慣用語

1. every man for himself   自求多福

哈哈：Not gonna make it. My boss will kill me.
來不及了，我老闆會殺了我的。

Lyla：Every man for himself. I've also got my deadlines to meet.
自求多福吧！我自己也有工作要趕。

2. Every man has his price. 沒有人是收買不了的

哈哈：He's not gonna jump ship. He's got everything he wanted there.

他不會跳槽的，他在那邊什麼都不缺啊！

Lyla：Every man has his price. Offer him more money.

沒有人是收買不了的，給他出更高的價碼。

3. a man of one's word 說到做到

哈哈：Trust me. I'm a man of my word.

相信我，我大丈夫一言既出，駟馬難追。

Lyla：I'm questioning the "man's" part.

我質疑的是「大丈夫」的部分。

4. new man 新好男人

哈哈：I'm going home. I need to bathe my little nephew.

我要回家了，我得幫我小外甥洗澡。

Lyla：You're such a new man.

你可真是個新好男人！

5. It's not the size of the man in the fight, it's the size of the fight in the man. 勝負的關鍵不在體型大小，而在志氣高低。

哈哈：Do I look like I have any chance to win? He's a retired NBA player!

妳覺得我有可能贏嗎？他是 NBA 退休選手欸！

Lyla：It's not the size of the man in the fight, it's the size of the fight in the man.

勝負的關鍵不在體型大小，而在志氣高低。

第 16 章 哈啦女人

角色：哈哈（來自台灣）、Lyla（來自美國）

假如你能和一個外國人 talk about girls「談論女孩子」，那你們一定是對好麻吉！但你認為談論女孩子一定得大聊外貌和肉體嗎？那可不見得！本章我們就來解鎖用英文聊女人的技能，讓你不只能聊得溜，也能聊得有深度。

1. She's hot! 她好正！

> hot 迷人的

「好正！」在英文裡的說法就是 hot 這個詞，比如：Oh my god! She's hot!「喔！天啊！她好正！」另外，我們還能說 She's a hottie.「她是個正妹。」、She's a cutie.「她真可愛。」其他表示「漂亮」的說法還有：You look stunning.、You look fabulous. 和 You look gorgeous.，這些都能表示「你看起來好美。」

• 關於「正妹」，你還能這樣說：

She's got a great body.
她的身材超讚！

She's a perfect ten.
她簡直完美！

She's a knockout!
她超正的！

body 身材	knockout 極為美麗的人

2. She's kinda wide.　她有點胖。

> wide　胖的

哪個男人沒有對女人的身材品頭論足過呢？現在我們就來學學除了 fat「胖」、thin「瘦」和 short「矮」之外，還有哪些比較道地的描述身材的詞彙。well-proportioned 表示「比例完美的」、curvy 表示「凹凸有致的」、well-endowed 和 well-developed 是委婉地表示「胸部大的」，而比較粗俗的説法是 booby。

- 關於「評論女人身材」，你還能這樣說：

She's straight up and down.
她的身材很平。

She's too skinny.
她太瘦了。

Look at that petite little girl.
看那個小隻女孩。

straight up and down　身材扁平的	skinny　瘦的	petite　嬌小的

3. Her face is getting round.　她的臉變圓了。

> round　圓的

除了身材之外，女人最常被討論的就是臉蛋了。要稱讚女孩子的「臉蛋很好看」，我們可以説：She's got a pretty face.；形容「臉變圓了」，我們會説：Her face is getting round.，而 You look really appealing with your hair down. 則是形容「你頭髮放下來真好看。」其中，appealing 是「吸引人的」的意思。另外，如果我們要説：「我很喜歡……」，除了 I like… 之外，還可以説：I'm attracted to...。

- 關於「女人外貌」，你還能這樣說：

She's got a cute face.

她的臉蛋很可愛。

Her teeth are a train wreck.
她的牙齒簡直像車禍現場。

I am attracted to women's eyes. They're captivating.
我會被女人的眼睛吸引，非常迷人。

wreck 失事	captivating 勾人的

4. She always spends hours getting dolled up in the morning.
她早上總是花好幾個小時打扮。

doll up 盛裝打扮

你身邊有沒有朋友是絕不能讓別人看到她素顏，或不化妝就不出門的呢？或者是妳自己就是這種人呢？這種「盛裝打扮」的行為，我們叫 get dolled up，如：
She spent almost an hour getting dolled up for the party.「她昨天為了要去派對花了將近一個小時打扮。」

• 關於「女人愛漂亮」，你還能這樣說：

She won't let anyone see her without makeup on.
她不化妝的時候絕對不會讓任何人看見。

A girl can never have too many clothes in her wardrobe.
女孩子衣櫃裡的衣服永遠不嫌多。

Don't you think she's overdressed herself?
你不覺得她穿得太誇張了嗎？

makeup 化妝	wardrobe 衣櫃	overdress 過度裝束

5. She's a bit of a tomboy. 她有一點男孩子氣。

tomboy 男孩子氣的女生

「男孩子氣的女生」，英文裡叫 tomboy 或 tomboyish，可能是某些人的 turn off「令人喪失興致的點」，卻也可能是某些人的 turn on「令人產生興致的點」。想想看，有哪些女生大剌剌的行為是你不能忍受的，有哪些是你覺得很迷人的呢？

- 關於「女生大剌剌」，你還能這樣說：

She's boyish.
她很男孩子氣。

Pink is never her color.
她受不了粉紅色。

She would just throw on a grungy T-shirt and baggy pants.
她都隨便穿件髒兮兮的 T 恤和寬鬆的褲子。

boyish 男孩子氣的	throw on 隨便穿上	grungy 髒兮兮的
baggy 寬鬆的		

6. If a woman's got a good personality, she's in the game.
如果一個女人的個性好，她就可能是我的菜。

personality 個性／ in the game 有機會成功

除了肉體外，還是有人追求女人的靈魂的。很多時候，外表一般的女生，如果擁有吸引人的內在，通常都會比漂亮女孩子更受歡迎喔！因此，除了長相之外，如果有人問你：What do you look for in a woman?「你看重女人的什麼？」你可以回答：It's all about her personality.「個性最重要。」或 Personality always comes first.「個性永遠擺第一。」、She's gotta have a good personality.「她的個性一定要很好。」

- 關於「女人真迷人」，你還能這樣說：

She's gotta have a beautiful smile.
她一定要有迷人的笑容。

A woman's brain is the sexiest part of her body.
女人的頭腦是她身上最性感的部位。

Loyalty, confidence and simplicity are definitely the biggest turn-ons for me.
專情、自信和簡單對我來說是最吸引人的點。

brain 頭腦	sexy 性感的	loyalty 忠誠
confidence 自信	simplicity 簡單	definitely 絕對
turn-on 吸引人的點		

7. She's quite high-maintenance. 她公主病挺嚴重的。

high-maintenance 有公主病的

英文中的 high-maintenance 是形容「需要花很多心思或金錢去照料的」物件或人，基本上可以作為「公主病」的同義詞。相反地，low-maintenance 就是指「不需要花太多心思或金錢去照料的人或東西」。另外，「公主病」我們還可以說：princess tendencies，如：She has serious princess tendencies.「她有很嚴重的公主病。」

• 關於「女生真麻煩」，你還能這樣說：

Why do girls always take so long to get ready?
為什麼女生出門前都要磨蹭那麼久？

She's a drama queen.
她很會鬧情緒。

It's that time of the month.
她大姨媽來了。

drama queen 情緒化的人

8. All women like romance.　所有女人都喜歡浪漫。

> romance 浪漫

很常聽到人說：「沒有女生喜歡……」和「沒有女生不喜歡……」這種話。雖然這種一概而論的論述在政治正確上都站不住腳，但也反映出還是有很多人都落入了這種大眾化的思維裡。現在，我們就來聊聊 All women like... 和 All women want... 吧！

• 關於「女人喜惡」，你還能這樣說：

Women want financial security in a relationship.
女人在一段關係中想要的是經濟上的安全感。

I want to have a life outside of dating. That is important to me.
我想要在談戀愛之餘也能擁有自己的生活，那對我來說很重要。

Women are attracted to men who lead.
女人會被有領導力的男人吸引。

financial 經濟的	security 安全	relationship 情感關係
dating 約會	attract 吸引	lead 領導

9. I like her assertiveness. She seems to radiate confidence when she speaks.　我喜歡她的自信，她講話的時候好像都在散發自信。

> assertiveness 自信／radiate 散發／confidence 自信

妳可曾仰慕或欣賞那種在職場上閃閃發光、超做自己的新時代女性呢？這種女生或多或少都會有點 feminist「女性主義者」的傾向，對於她們來說，所謂的 sexism「性別主義」、misogyny「女性貶義」和 male chauvinism「男性沙文主義」都屬於很嚴重的歧視思想。在這個時代，人們的認知逐漸開闊，正義和真理逐漸越辯越明，是否「新女性」這個詞能因為理性和包容性普及於每個人，從而失去意義呢？

- 關於「新女性」，你還能這樣說：

She sounds like a feminist.
她聽起來像個女性主義者。

Men and women should be treated equally.
男人和女人應該被平等地對待。

We women should stand up for ourselves.
我們女人應該要為自己站出來。

feminist 女性主義者	treat 對待	equally 平等地
stand up for oneself 為自己站出來		

10. Girls are supposed to be feminine.　女孩子就是要女孩子氣一點。

> be supposed to 應該要／ feminine 女性化的

雖然每個人都是獨立的個體，There's no point in saying you're a girl and you're a boy.「老是說：『妳是個女孩子，你是個男孩子』是沒有意義的。」但現實世界中，還是有很多這種害人匪淺的固化思想，讓我們來看看以下的句子你聽過哪些吧！

- 關於「女人應該要」，你還能這樣說：

Hey! You are a girl!
嘿！妳可是個女孩子欸！

Some people think women are just baby-making machines.
有些人覺得女人就是生孩子的機器。

Women should just be at home, have kids.
女人就應該待在家，生小孩。

machine 機器

1. as cute as a button　超可愛

哈哈：I like Lisa. She's as cute as a button.
我喜歡 Lisa，她超可愛的。

Lyla：Don't even think about her. She's off the market.
她你就別想了，她死會了。

2. a woman for all seasons　全能的女人

哈哈：Katrina sings, plays the piano and speaks five languages. She's so amazing!
Katrina 會唱歌、會彈鋼琴，還會說五種語言，她好厲害啊！

Lyla：She's indeed a woman for all seasons.
她真的是個全能的女人。

3. A woman is as old as she admits.　女人的年紀她們說的算

哈哈：Do you know how old Halsey is?
妳知道 Halsey 幾歲嗎？

Lyla：You know...a woman is as old as she admits.
你知道……女人的年紀都他們說的算。

4. badge bunny　迷戀穿（警察）制服的女人

哈哈：Have you noticed Emma only goes out with policemen?
妳有發現 Emma 只跟警察交往嗎？

Lyla：Yes. She's a typical badge bunny.
有啊！她就是所謂的徽章兔子吧！

5. a woman among women　傑出的女人

哈哈：I really admire Ashley's leadership. She's a woman among
women.

我好欣賞 Ashley 的領導能力，她是位傑出的女人。

Lyla：Well...She's my boss, so I'd rather not make any comment about
her.

嗯……她是我上司，所以我還是不要評論她什麼比較好。

第17章 哈啦談戀愛

角色：哈哈（來自台灣）、Lyla（來自美國）

「愛是種責任」、「愛是不保留」、「愛很簡單」、「愛是種近乎幻想的真理」，流行樂歌頌了許多愛，但很多人還是搞不懂「愛是個什麼東西」，不過沒關係，先別想這麼多，「愛了就知道」了！本章節，我們就一起來「談戀愛」吧！

1. Are you guys...? 你們是不是……？

> **you guys 你們**

「曖昧讓人受盡委屈」，但曖昧也是整段戀愛關係中最青澀，也最令人神魂顛倒的階段了。雖然我們平時看英美影集時，總覺得他們的進展速度都令人傻眼地快，但他們其實還是會有曖昧階段的。而「曖昧」在英文中，最貼切的詞應該就是 chemistry 了，比如：You two had chemistry.「你們兩個有點曖昧。」，這裡的 chemistry 指的就是兩人之間的「化學反應」。另外，也可以說：I can see there's something between you and her.「我看得出來你和她之間有點曖昧。」如果你想委婉一點，不想一語道破的話，你可以這樣問：Are you guys...?「你們是不是……？」如果對方招供的話，可以說：Yeah...a little bit.「嗯……有一點吧！」

- 關於「曖昧」，你還能這樣說：

  Is there anything between you and Sophie?
  你跟 Sophie 之間有什麼嗎？

  We're talking.
  我們在曖昧中。

  I can see there's chemistry between you guys.
  我可以感覺到你們之間有曖昧的火花。

> **chemistry 化學**

2. I'm so deep in the friend zone.　她真的只把我當朋友。

> deep 深的／ friendzone 朋友區

中文説的「發好人卡」，在英文中有一個很有意思的對應是 friendzone「置於朋友區」，如：I'm going to friendzone him.「我要發他好人卡。」意思是讓對方無法進入到戀人關係的領域，而 being so deep in the friendzone 就是深陷於朋友區，無法脱身了。這種朋友，我們也可以説：He's a just friend.「他只是朋友。」

- 關於「戀人未滿」，你還能這樣說：

I get awkward around him.
我跟他在一起時有點尷尬。

I like her as a friend.
我對她只是朋友的喜歡。

That didn't go anywhere.
那並沒有什麼進展。

> awkward 尷尬的

3. He asked me out!　他約我出去了！

> ask someone out 約⋯⋯出去

「追求」某人千萬不能用 follow ！最簡單的説法是 ask someone out「約某人出去」或 pursue「追求」。一群男生聚在一起的時候，經常會互相拱某人：Come on! Ask her out!「快去約她！」

- 關於「追求」，你還能這樣說：

Should I pursue her?
我該追求她嗎？

I've been running after the girl for nearly a year.
我追了這個女孩子將近一年了。

Wooing a girl is an art.
追求女孩子是門藝術。

pursue 追求	run after 追求	nearly 將近
woo 追求	art 藝術	

4. I told my crush I like her. 我跟我喜歡的人告白了。

crush 喜歡的對象

crush 這個詞的原意是「壓碎」，當名詞時則有「暗戀」的意思，如：I have a crush on her.「我喜歡她。」另外，也可以當「暗戀對象」，如：I finally told my crush I like her.「我終於跟我喜歡的人告白了。」

• 關於「告白」，你還能這樣說：

Should I confess my love to her?
我應該向她表白嗎？

I wrote him a confession letter.
我寫給他一封告白信。

I told her my feelings.
我跟她告白了。

confess 告白	confession letter 告白信	feelings 情感

5. They've been going out for about a year.

他們已經交往大概一年了。

go out 約會

「交往」、「在一起」常見的說法有：date、see each other 和 be together，其實，還有一個更簡單的說法是 go out，如：They've been going out for about a year.「他們已經交往大概一年了。」或 She's been going out with Tom.「她最近和 Tom 在交往。」

• 關於「交往」，你還能這樣說：

We've been together for three years.

我們交往三年了。

How long have you been seeing each other?

你們交往多久了？

How long have you been dating Lucy?

你跟 Lucy 交往多久了？

see each other 交往	date 約會

6. She's in a relationship.　她談戀愛了。

relationship 情侶關係

電影《情人節快樂》中的一句台詞：I can be a sappy cheeseball all day.「我可以整天風花雪月、多愁善感。」非常適合用來形容戀愛中的男女粉紅泡泡滿頭飛的模樣。如果你身旁有人出現這種跡象，你便能問他：Are you in love?「你談戀愛了嗎？」

• 關於「戀愛中」，你還能這樣說：

Are you in love?

你談戀愛了嗎？

I fell in love with him.
我愛上他了。

Leave the lovestruck couple alone.
別打擾那對熱戀中的情侶了。

fall in love 愛上	leave alone 不打擾	lovestruck 熱戀中的

7. I can always talk to him. He's always there for me.
我永遠都能找他聊心事，他也永遠都會守護著我。

> be there for someone 守護某人

所謂 Beauty is in the eye of the beholder.「情人眼裡出西施。」戀愛中的男女不只在對方的眼中是最帥最美的，由於愉悅的心情和每天吃好睡好，整個人真的會容光煥發呢！除此之外，他們成天掛在嘴邊的不是晚上要去哪裡約會，就是對方多麼地好、多麼地體貼，blablabla... 來看看有哪些幸福洋溢的戀愛話語吧！

• 關於「戀愛中的話語」，你還能這樣說：

I love the way he looks at me.
我喜歡他看著我的樣子。

He makes me think I'm the best person in the world.
他讓我覺得我是這個世界上最棒的人。

He can always make me smile.
他總是能讓我笑。

smile 微笑

8. We spent three years in a long-distance relationship.

我們有三年的時間都在談遠距離戀愛。

> long-distance　遠距離的

戀愛中也有分成很多階段，包含尷尬期、熱戀期、磨合期、穩定期、老夫老妻期等，很多人甚至可能因為個性、習慣和各種現實原因而進入冷靜期，甚至是分分合合的狀態。而這些戀愛狀態該如何描述呢？一起來看看吧！

- 關於「各種戀愛狀態」，你還能這樣說：

Go get a room!
去開房間啦！

He started going steady with Joanna.
他開始和 Joanna 穩定交往。

I'm tired of this on-again-off-again relationship.
我受夠了這種分分合合的戀情。

steady　穩定的	on-again-off-again　分分合合的

9. He dumped me.　他把我甩了。

> dump　丟棄

人生不過短短幾十個寒暑，人與人之間也如萍水相逢，聚散有時。更何況是談感情有如兩個獨立的宇宙圍繞彼此旋轉，彼此原生的差異加上現實的摩擦力，若無法磨合便無法順利旋轉下去，那倒不如還彼此自由，好聚好散。因此，談戀愛自然會需要聊到「談分手」啦！關於「分手」，我們可以這樣說：This is not working out.「我們走不下去了。」、I'm leaving you.「我要離開你。」、Let's just be friends.「我們還是當朋友吧！」

- 關於「分手」，你還能這樣說：

They broke up.
他們分手了。

We couldn't work out our differences, so I decided to end it.

我們無法解決彼此間的不同，所以我決定分手了。

I'm done with Ian.

我和 Ian 玩完了。

break up 分手	work out 解決	difference 差異
end 結束	done 結束了的	

10. I would still purposely avoid all those places and things.

我還是會刻意迴避那些地方和東西。

purposely 刻意地／ avoid 避免

談戀愛失敗非常正常，分手也在所難免，雖然戀愛時的各種足跡都可能成為分手後的雷區，但我們還是要對人生、對愛情抱有希望，勇敢去愛，用心付出，才不負此生，不是嗎？最後，我們一起來學學如何表達分手後的各種心情。

• 關於「分手後」，你還能這樣說：

I miss everything about her.

我想念她的一切。

I still haven't got over my ex.

我還沒放下我前男友。

I want him back.

我想和他復合。

get over 放下；釋懷	ex 前任男女朋友

1. have butterflies in one's stomach　小鹿亂撞

哈哈：I have butterflies in my stomach whenever I talk to Chloe.
我每次跟 Chloe 講話時都覺得小鹿亂撞。

Lyla：You have a crush on her.
你喜歡上她了。

2. head over heels　神魂顛倒

哈哈：Nina is so boy crazy! I'm sure she's gonna fall for my friend Alex when she meets him.
Nina 真是個花癡，我覺得她見到我朋友 Alex 的時候肯定會愛上他。

Lyla：Head over heels!
肯定神魂顛倒。

3. the apple of my eye　我眼中的唯一

哈哈：Lyla, you are the apple of my eye.
Lyla，妳是我眼中的唯一。

Lyla：You need to get your eyes checked up.
你該去看眼科了。

4. PDA（Public Display of Affection）　放閃

哈哈：Are you sure you're gonna invite Hester and Brady? They're always acting lovey-dovey! So annoying!
妳確定妳要邀 Hester 和 Brady 嗎？他們老是卿卿我我，好煩啊！

Lyla：I have no problem with PDAs.
放閃我還好啦！

5. a match made in heaven　天生一對

哈哈：Wait, Julie and Brad got married? Finally!
等等，Julie 和 Brad 結婚了？終於！

Lyla：They're indeed a match made in heaven.
他們確實很登對。

第 18 章　哈啦結婚

角色：哈哈（來自台灣）、Lyla（來自美國）

你到了被喜帖轟炸的年紀了嗎？或是這幾年過年時被親戚催婚了呢？當你開始認真思考是否該進入婚姻時，你可能會需要和別人聊聊婚姻內外的各種事，包含：求婚、訂婚、單身趴、宴客、蜜月，甚至婚姻問題、小三、離婚等。現在，不管你有沒有要結婚，看完這章後，在婚姻這檔事上，你一定能跟別人聊上幾句。

1. I'll put a ring on her finger faster than she can blink.
我會在她反應過來之前幫她戴上戒指。

ring 戒指／ blink 眨眼

即便到今天，婚戒還是很多人求婚時的必備信物。如果有人跟你說 I will put a ring on her finger. 那他的意思就是「我想娶她。」啦！而這句 I'll put a ring on her finger faster than she can blink. 「我會在她能眨眼之前就幫她帶上戒指。」是一句搞笑、誇大的說法，表示真的真的很想娶對方。

• 關於「求婚」，你還能這樣說：

I proposed to her.
我跟她求婚了。

So, when are you gonna pop the question?
所以你什麼時候要跟她求婚？

I think it's time we settled down.
我覺得我們是時候定下來了。

propose 求婚	pop 提出	settle down 安頓下來

2. I'm getting married.　我要結婚了。

get married 結婚

marry 這個詞是指「娶」或「嫁」，一般是這樣用的：I will marry him.「我願意嫁給他。」Will you marry me?「妳願意嫁給我嗎？」而「結婚」在英文中一般

是用 get married 表示結婚的「行為」，而 be married 則是表示結婚的「狀態」，如：They got married last month.「他們上個月結婚了。」和 They've been married for 10 years.「他們已經結婚十年了。」當然，結婚還有很多種說法，一起繼續看下去吧！

- 關於「結婚」，你還能這樣說：

I can't believe you're getting hitched.
我真不敢相信你要結婚了。

Marry that girl.
娶了她吧！

They're planning to tie the knot this summer.
他們計畫今年夏天結婚。

| get hitched 結婚 | marry 娶；嫁 | tie the knot 結婚 |

3. We'll throw you a bachelor party.　我們會幫你辦一場單身派對。

throw 舉辦／bachelor 單身漢

bachelor party 或 stag party「單身派對」是指男人在結婚前和自己的男性朋友一起舉辦的狂歡趴，一方面慶祝自己即將步入人生的另一階段，一方面則是把握最後的單身時光，盡情瘋狂。電影 The Hangover「醉後大丈夫」的第一集就是在講述一群好哥兒們在拉斯維加斯的單身派對上爛醉狂歡而發生的荒謬故事。當然，男人有 bachelor party，女人當然也有女人的單身派對囉！英文就叫 bachelorette party 或 bridal shower。

- 關於「結婚前後」，你還能這樣說：

We're gonna have ourselves a wild stag do in Vegas.
我們要在拉斯維加斯為自己舉辦一場瘋狂的單身派對。

I got a bridal shower invitation.
我收到新娘單身派對的邀請了。

We're going to Paris for our honeymoon.

我們要去巴黎度蜜月。

wild 狂野的	stag do 新郎單身派對	Vegas 拉斯維加斯
bridal shower 新娘單身派對	invitation 邀請	honeymoon 蜜月

4. We are going to have a religious ceremony.

我們打算要舉行宗教儀式的婚禮。

religious 宗教的／ceremony 典禮

不管在哪個國家，結婚都是一個非常繁瑣而複雜的過程。包含中西方都有的 proposal「求婚」、engagement ceremony「訂婚儀式」和 wedding ceremony「結婚儀式」。而結婚儀式依地點又分可成 church wedding「教堂婚禮」和 civil ceremony「公證結婚」兩種主要的形式。完成 wedding ceremony 之後，通常還需要再辦一個娛樂親友的 reception「宴客」。至於華人社會普遍存在的「聘金」和「嫁妝」分別是 bride price 和 dowry。西方一般沒有 bride price 的概念，但如果說 dowry 的話一般人都能理解的。

• 關於「婚禮」，你還能這樣說：

When's the big day?

婚禮什麼時候辦？

We'll have a big reception later.

我們之後會有大型宴客活動。

I'm not too fussed about holding a wedding reception.

我沒有一定得辦婚禮宴客不可。

big day 婚禮	reception 婚禮宴客	fussed 大驚小怪的
hold 舉行		

5. They've been happily married for 20 years.

他們已經結婚二十年了，到現在還是很幸福。

> happily 幸福地

祝福別人有一段美好的婚姻，我們會說 Happy marriage。而在婚姻中如何達到真正地快樂呢？這答案恐怕翻閱了幾萬篇博士論文都找不著吧！但也許能從他們平時的炫耀文中看出一些端倪喔！

• 關於「美好的婚姻」，你還能這樣說：

They just celebrated their 15th anniversary.
他們剛慶祝他們的十五週年紀念日。

We're gonna renew our vows this spring.
我們今年春天還要重申我們婚禮的誓言。

They complemented each other.
他們彼此互補。

celebrate 慶祝	anniversary 週年紀念	renew 重申
vow 誓言	complement 補足	

6. Obviously our relationship is going nowhere.

我們的關係顯然不會有任何結果。

> obviously 顯然地／relationship 情感關係／nowhere 無處

「婚姻觸礁」最貼切的說法是 on the rocks，如：My marriage is on the rocks. 「我的婚姻出了點問題。」其他的說法還有：Our marriage is not working out. 「我們的婚姻走不下去了。」、My marriage is failing. 「我的婚姻快不行了。」、My marriage is in trouble. 「我的婚姻有狀況。」或 Our relationship is going nowhere. 「我們的關係不會有任何結果。」觸礁的婚姻，可能會需要婚姻諮商，而「婚姻諮商」的英文是 marriage counseling。

- 關於「婚姻觸礁」，你還能這樣說：

Their marriage is on the rocks.
他們的婚姻觸礁了。

Their marriage has gone through a rough patch lately.
他們的婚姻最近出現了一些問題。

They've gone on holiday trying to patch up their relationship.
他們去度假了，試圖藉此挽救他們的關係。

marriage 婚姻	on the rocks 觸礁	go through a rough patch 遭遇問題
lately 最近	go on holiday 去度假	patch up 修補

7. He had an affair.　他外遇了。

affair 婚外情

所謂的「婚外情」在英文中我們會用 affair 或 extramarital relationship 來表示。至於大家口中常說的「小三」，男生會用 lover「情夫」，女生則是 mistress「情婦」。其他說法像是 the other man 和 the other woman、side guy 和 side bitch，或男女通用的 side piece，比如：She's tired of being a side piece.「她厭倦了當別人的小三。」

- 關於「婚外情」，你還能這樣說：

I never thought I would become the other woman.
我從來沒有想過自己會變成小三。

She caught her husband cheating with his co-worker.
她抓到她老公和他同事搞外遇。

She admitted she was unfaithful to her husband.
她承認她對她丈夫不忠。

the other woman 情婦	catch 抓到	cheat 欺騙
co-worker 同事	admit 承認	unfaithful 不忠的

8. She wants a divorce. 她想要離婚。

> divorce 離婚

最近有一個說法是：在戶政事務所登記離婚的隊伍比登記結婚的還多得多，非常誇張、非常形象化，但也顯示出現代社會的離婚率真是嚇死人的高。雖然很多人建議夫妻永遠不要把離婚提為一個協商的選項，但退一步看，不幸福的婚姻，不過像是進入一間不適合的公司，與其在裡面掙扎、苟且，不如果斷辭職，海闊天空，不是嗎？

• 關於「離婚」，你還能這樣說：

We parted on good terms.
我們是和平離婚的。

So many marriages end in divorce nowadays.
現在好多婚姻都以離婚收場。

His parents broke up when he was in high school.
他父母在他讀高中時離婚了。

part 分開	on good terms 和平地；友善地	marriage 婚姻
end in 以……收場	nowadays 現今	break up 分手

9. I have commitment issues. 我有承諾恐懼症。

> commitment 承諾／ issue 問題

你有一群大齡剩男剩女的朋友嗎？如果你和他們聊起婚姻，他們可能會以各種瀟灑的論調擺弄這個話題，但當你走進他們的內心，你可能會聽到各種聲音都環繞不出某些特定的詞彙。其中，最常聽到的可能就是 I have commitment issues.「我有承諾恐懼症。」或 I am afraid of commitment.「我害怕給出承諾。」

• 關於「恐婚症」，你還能這樣說：

She just spends too much time nitpicking.
她就是太挑了。

I still feel scarred from the previous relationship.

我還沒走出上一段感情的傷痛。

She ends up keeping everyone at an arm's length.

她後來就一直拒人於千里之外。

| nitpick 吹毛求疵 | scar 留下傷痕 | previous 先前的 |
| end up 結果 | keep someone at an arm's length
拒絕與人深交 | |

10. Marriage is a two-way street. 婚姻是互相的。

> two-way street 互相的;有施有受的

婚姻生活有苦有樂,在裡在外的風景有如兩個世界,白天不懂夜的黑,夜也不懂白日的明媚。在外的人,可能會發覺在裡面的人給出的忠告有著令人驚訝的一致性,直到當自己步入其中時,才驚覺原來那些陳腔濫調還真是其來有自的。一起來看看有哪些逆耳的忠言吧!

• 關於「婚姻忠告」,你還能這樣說:

Never get married.

千萬別結婚。

Marriage is the tomb of love.

婚姻是愛情的墳墓。

The grass is greener where you water it.

所有的婚姻關係都是需要經營的。

| tomb 墳墓 | grass 草 | water 澆水 |

1. get down on one knee　下跪求婚

哈哈：What would you do if your boyfriend got down on one knee at a crowded concert?

如果妳男朋友在滿滿都是人的演唱會上下跪求婚妳會怎麼樣？

Lyla：I would run away. That's too embarrassing.

我會逃走，那太尷尬了！

2. take the plunge　下定決心結婚

哈哈：Leo is hesitant about if he should marry Linda.

Leo 還在猶豫要不要和 Linda 結婚。

Lyla：He shouldn't take the plunge if he's not ready.

他如果還沒準備好就不應該現在決定。

3. walk down the aisle　步入禮堂

Lyla：I can't picture myself walking down the aisle someday.

我無法想像自己步入禮堂的那一天。

哈哈：I can't imagine someone would be willing to suffer.

我也無法想像有人會這麼想不開。

4. get cold feet　臨陣脫逃

哈哈：What would you do if your boyfriend got cold feet on your wedding day?

如果妳男朋友在你們婚禮當天臨陣脫逃，妳怎麼辦？

Lyla：I think I'm more likely to get cold feet.

我覺得我自己更有可能會臨陣脫逃吧！

5. shot gun wedding　奉子成婚

哈哈：A little bird told me that Cynthia had been pregnant before she got married.

有小道消息説 Cynthia 在結婚前就懷孕了欸！

Lyla：Wow! So that was a shot gun wedding, wasn't it?

哇！所以她是奉子成婚囉！

第19章 哈啦小孩

角色：哈哈（來自台灣）、Lyla（來自美國）

Are you a kid person?「你喜歡小孩子嗎？」Are you good with kids?「你對小孩子很有一套嗎？」Or you can't stand children?「或者你受不了小孩子呢？」從定義上來看，所謂的「成人」就是距離孩童時期有一定時日的人，當他們聊起小孩時，有人開心到融化，有人卻聞風喪膽。不管怎樣，小孩的確是世界上非常獨特的一群生物，甚至擁有一套獨特的語言系統呢！不信的話，一起來聊聊吧！

1. We're expecting a baby. 我們快要有小孩子了。

expect 預期

expect 意思是「期待」、「預期」，放到 We're expecting a baby. 這個語境中便是「快要有」的意思。而在另一個句子 Are we expecting anyone? 中的 expect 則表示「即將迎接」，因此，整句的意思便是「等一下有客人要來嗎？」expect 還可以延伸出 expectant 這個形容詞，表示「準⋯⋯」，因此，「準爸爸」和「準媽媽」便是 expectant father 和 expectant mother。

• 關於「生小孩」，你還能這樣說：

She's pregnant.
她懷孕了。

Are you gonna have kids?
你們要生小孩嗎？

We have an expectant father here.
我們這裡有一位準爸爸喔！

pregnant 懷孕的	expectant 即將生孩子的

2. Did you see Adam's new born baby? 　你看到 Adam 的小嬰兒了嗎？

new born 新生的／ baby 嬰兒

baby、kid 和 child 都可以指「小孩」，但他們究竟有什麼差別呢？ baby 是指剛出生的「嬰兒」，可被用來引申為「長不大的人」，如：Don't be a baby.「別像個小孩一樣。」kid 和 child 都是指比 baby 大的小孩，其中，kid 比較口語，語氣較親暱，而 child 比較正式，語氣較中性。另外一個詞 toddler 則是指「在學走路的小孩」，是由 toddle「蹣跚行走」這個動詞變化得來的。

- 關於「各種小孩」，你還能這樣說：

She's the youngest child.
她是老么。

He's a preemie.
他是個早產兒。

He's not an ordinary ten-year-old kid.
他不是一個普通的十歲小孩。

preemie 早產兒	ordinary 普通的

3. His cheeks are so soft. 　他的臉蛋好軟喔！

cheeks 臉頰

你喜歡捏捏小孩嗎？尤其是剛出生不久的嬰兒，有如剛出爐的香噴噴的饅頭一樣，可口又可愛！這個時候，旁邊的家人通常會來一句：「喜歡就自己生一個啊！」殊不知，喜歡捏小孩和自己養小孩是兩回事啊！

- 關於「嬰兒」，你還能這樣說：

Her tiny little hands and feet are just sooo cute.
她的小手手小腳丫真的超可愛的。

Oh, I love the new baby smell.
噢！我好喜歡這種嬰兒的香味。

She's so tiny!
她好小隻喔！

tiny 小的

4. He might have a wet diaper.　他可能尿尿了。

wet 濕的／diaper 尿布

養小孩不是養寵物，嗯……但有時候，養小孩就是像在養寵物啊！你曾用百般佩服的眼神看著你的新手爸媽朋友，讚嘆他們是如何知道小孩是因為肚子餓在哭還是想睡覺在哭的嗎？然而，當你看著他們嫻熟的動作和滿溢的父愛／母愛，你想：也許……還是先養隻寵物練練吧！

• 關於「嬰兒的生理需求」，你還能這樣說：

How do you burp a baby?
要怎麼幫嬰兒拍嗝？

I breastfed both of my kids.
我兩個小孩都是餵哺母乳的。

How do I know if it's a hunger cry or a sleep cry?
我怎麼知道他哭是因為餓了還是睏了？

burp 拍嗝	breastfeed 餵哺母乳	hunger 飢餓

5. I've never held a baby before.　我沒抱過小孩。

> hold　拿著；抱著

英文有時候比中文要囉唆得多，分得也比中文細。如：「抱」的中文就一個詞，但在英文中卻分成 hug「短暫擁抱」、cuddle「長時間地、親密地抱」和 hold「用手抱著」。而「抱小孩」呢，一般會用 hold 這個詞。我們可以 hold a bag、hold a package、hold 任何東西，而 hold a baby 就像抱著一個小東西一樣，自然就用 hold 這個詞囉！抱小孩時，我們還可能會説到：hold him up against you「把他抱起來靠著你」、Is it too much?「會太大力嗎？」、Do I flip her around?「我要換邊抱嗎？」

• 關於「接觸小孩」，你還能這樣說：

She's not afraid of you.
她不怕你。

She just keeps wiggling around.
她一直動來動去。

You can also rock him a little bit.
你還可以輕輕搖他一下。

afraid　害怕的	wiggle　蠕動	rock　搖晃

6. Hello! Little cutey!　哈囉！小可愛！

> cutey　可愛的

baby talk「兒童語言」其實不難，三個原則：第一，尾音加上 y，如：cutey、mommy、doggy；第二，運用兩遍單音節詞，如：dinner 説成 din din、bottle 説成 baba、bye 説成 bye bye；第三，重複 baby 説的話，不管嬰兒説什麼，重複一遍就對了！

• 關於「兒童語言」，你還能這樣說：

Time for din din!
吃晚飯囉！

Baby want the baba?

小寶貝想要喝水水嗎？

Yum yum! Eat some more!

好吃好吃！再吃一點！

din din 晚餐	**baba** 水瓶	**yum yum** 好吃的

7. What grade are you in? 你幾年級了？

> grade 年級

很多人發現自己不怎麼會跟小孩子交流，這些人常犯的錯誤一般是過猶不及，也就是太把他們當成小孩子了，用了太多的 baby talk「兒童語言」，殊不知小孩子常常比我們想像得更成熟，懂得更多。其實，和小孩子溝通只需要用正常的語言，多站在他們角度思考，一般都會很順利的。這邊我們來聊聊幾句常見的和小孩交流的話題。

- 關於「與小孩互動」，你還能這樣說：

How many brothers and sisters do you have?

你有幾個兄弟姊妹？

What do you like to do for fun?

你平時喜歡做什麼？

Do you have any pets?

你有養寵物嗎？

fun 樂趣	**pet** 寵物

8. My son has hit the terrible twos.　我兒子已經到可怕的兩歲反抗期了。

> hit the terrible twos　到了兩歲反抗期

很多小孩都是大人眼中的 little monsters「小怪獸」，不是在親戚家爬上爬下、就是撕紙、拆家具等，各種脫序。但話說回來，如果小孩子個個都是通情達理、文質彬彬的，想起來也挺嚇人的，不是嗎？一起來看看小怪獸們的各種症狀用英文怎麼說。

• 關於「小孩真麻煩」，你還能這樣說：

You see what I'm dealing with?
你看到我有多傷腦筋了吧？

He's going through a little rebellious phase.
他正經歷小小的叛逆期。

I didn't know middle child syndrome was a real thing.
我以前不知道中間兒童綜合症真的存在。

deal with　處理	go through　經歷	rebellious　叛逆的
phase　階段	middle child　中間兒童	syndrome　綜合症

9. You've grown so big.　你長好大了。

> grow　成長

我們可能都很熟悉所謂的三姑六婆、親戚朋友議論各自的小孩時各種誇、各種嫌的場景吧！不要以為這種場景不會在國外上演喔！西方人也會有三姑六婆說南道北的，只是因為他們是西方人，所以我們自動把這個標籤撕掉罷了。而他們議論小孩時，也不出那幾個話題，如：You've grown so big!「你長好大了！」、He's so precocious.「他好早熟喔！」、He's at the top of his class.「他在班上都是前幾名的。」等。

• 關於「議論小孩」，你還能這樣說：

He has your eyes.
他的眼睛很像你。

I always have a soft spot for him.

我總是比較偏愛他。

They behaved themselves?

他們還乖嗎？

have a soft spot for someone 偏愛某人	
behave oneself 表現地守規矩	

10. I'm not a huge baby person.　我不太喜歡小孩子。

huge 巨大的／ baby person 喜歡小孩的人

I'm afraid of babies.「我很怕小孩子。」、He doesn't enjoy my presence.「他不喜歡我在這。」I'm gonna make him cry.「我會把他弄哭。」如果你有小孩恐懼症，你可能會需要這幾個句子！不勉強，也許不愛小孩就像不愛吃香菜一樣，是基因造成的吧！

• 關於「小孩恐懼症」，你還能這樣說：

I'm not around a lot of babies.

我沒接觸過很多小孩子。

I suck at babysitting.

我超不會照顧小孩的。

Babies don't normally mess with me.

小孩子一般不太跟我玩。

around 與……為伍	**suck** 遜	**babysitting** 褓母工作
normally 一般而言	**mess with** 和……玩耍	

1. sleep like a baby　睡得很香

哈哈：Why didn't you call me? I missed the wedding!
妳怎麼沒有打給我？我錯過婚禮了！

Lyla：I did. But you were probably sleeping like a baby then.
我打了，但你那時候大概睡得正香吧！

2. kid stuff　容易至極

Lyla：I ran ten miles last night. I was exhausted!
我昨晚跑了十英里，快累死了！

哈哈：Ten miles? That's kid stuff!
十英里？太容易了吧！

3. babe in the woods　不知世故的人

哈哈：I'm still concerned about you accepting that offer.
妳要做那份工作，我還是有點擔心。

Lyla：I'm not a babe in the woods! I know what I'm doing!
我又不是什麼都不懂，我知道我自己在做什麼！

4. Children and fools tell the truth.　小孩和傻子淨說大實話。

哈哈：I was so mortified when John said my boss's mouth stank.
John 說我老闆的嘴巴很臭的時候，我簡直尷尬死了。

Lyla：Children and fools tell the truth!
小孩和傻子淨說大實話啊！

5. Children should be seen and not heard.　小孩子不該亂講話。

哈哈：Lyla, you seem to have gained weight.
Lyla，妳好像胖了。

Lyla：Children should be seen and not heard!
小孩子別亂講話！

第 20 章 哈啦吵架

角色：哈哈（來自台灣）、Lyla（來自美國）

有人吵架時，頭腦清晰、語速逼人；有人吵架時則是氣急敗壞、話都講不清楚。試想：如果自己是用英文吵架，而英文又不太溜時，那可真是有苦說不出，只能把滿肚子的氣憋回去了。本章節就來教你如何用英文吵架，幫你在對抗老外時提高自己的「戰鬥力」！

1. You'd better have it out with her.　你最好跟她講清楚。

had better　最好／ have it out with　和……講清楚

fight 不只有「打架」的意思，也可以用來指「吵架」。因此，「怎樣？想吵架啊？」在英文中，我們可以說：You wanna fight? 或 You wanna pick a fight?，其中 pick a fight 字面上就是「挑起爭端」的意思。另外，have it out with someone 的意思則是「和……講清楚」，通常是對方做了令你生氣的事，你想找對方講清楚時可以用。

• 關於「開啟爭端」，你還能這樣說：

You wanna take this outside?
你想外面解決嗎？

You wanna pick a fight?
你想吵架是不是？

We need to talk.
我們需要談談。

take this outside　外面解決	pick a fight　挑起爭端

2. We had a major fight.　我們大吵了一架。

major　大型的／ fight　吵架

英文中的「吵架」分幾種：spat 是「小吵架」，通常是針對微不足道的瑣事、argument 是指「爭論」，通常是針對某個客觀的議題的意見來往、quarrel 是指「熟人之間的爭吵」，通常帶有更多的無理和情緒化，而 fight 則是最廣義的「吵

架」或「打架」。如果要表示「大吵一架」，我們可以說：We had a major fight.「我們大吵了一架。」

- 關於「吵架」，你還能這樣說：

We just had a spat.
我們只是小吵架。

We had an argument.
我們吵架了。

We fight a lot.
我們很常吵架。

spat 小爭執	argument 爭論

3. You're getting on my nerves.　你惹毛我了。

get on one's nerves 惹毛某人

「惹某人生氣」，除了 make someone angry 之外，我們還可以說 piss someone off 或 tick someone off。在非常口語的場合甚至還可以說 PO，如：Your dad is already POed.「你爸已經生氣了。」此外，upset 和 mad 也很常用來表示「生氣」，如：Is he mad at something?「他在生氣嗎？」而 get on one's nerves 字面上的意思是「爬上某人的神經」，也可以很形象地描述生氣的意思。

- 關於「惹人生氣」，你還能這樣說：

Aggravating!
你真的讓人很火大！

I'm still pissed off about the stunt you pulled yesterday.
我還在生你昨天惡作劇弄我的氣。

Is he upset with you?
他在生你的氣嗎？

aggravating 令人生氣的	piss off 使生氣	pull a stunt 惡作劇
upset 生氣的		

4. Don't you dare!　你敢！

> dare　敢

Don't you dare!「你敢！」這句話可以用在類似這種情況：Lyla：I'm gonna call your mom and tell her everything!「我要打給你媽，把所有的事都告訴她。」哈哈：Don't you dare!「你敢！」而另一個很常搞混的是 I dare you! 表示「諒你也不敢！」，比如：Lyla：I'm gonna ask him out!「我要去約他！」哈哈：I dare you!「我賭你不敢！」可以看得出來 Don't you dare! 的語氣比較憤怒而強烈，而 I dare you! 則是表達一種挑釁的不信任感，加強語氣時還可以說：I double dare you!「我真的笑你不敢！」

• 關於「撂狠話」，你還能這樣說：

Stop being a pussy! Grow a pair!
別孬了！有種一點好嗎！

You don't want to say that again! You hear me?
你最好不要再說一遍！聽到了沒？

You so much as step inside the room, you will be sorry!
你要是敢踏進這間房間一步，你就慘了！

pussy 小貓	grow 長	so much as 甚至
step 踏	sorry 遺憾的	

5. Get lost!　滾！

> lost 走失的

真正生氣的時候講出的氣話，那真是要多難聽有多難聽！這邊我們就來學學幾句殺傷力比較小的氣話，讓自己生氣的時候有點解氣的效果吧！其中，叫別人「滾」，最髒的可能是 fxxk off，而如果你想要語不帶髒字的話，可以說 get lost 或 take a hike。

- 關於「氣話」，你還能這樣說：

I don't give a damn.
我一點都不在乎。

I'm so fed up with your bullshit.
我受夠了你的廢話。

I'm disgusted by you.
我好討厭你。

fed up 受夠了的	bullshit 胡說	disgust 使厭惡

6. Do not bad mouth me.　不要罵我髒話。

bad mouth 罵髒話

當然，吵架的時候不帶髒字的確不太現實，但當對方對我們口出穢言時，我們不見得也要以髒話回應，有時候用其他的方式酸回去還更能體現自己的格調，進而幫助自己在吵架過程中取得上風呢！來學學有哪些罵人不帶髒字的反擊話吧！

- 關於「罵髒話」，你還能這樣說：

You eat with that mouth?
你用那張嘴吃飯的嗎？

Watch your mouth!
注意你的嘴！

Don't you swear at me!
不要對我罵髒話！

watch 注意	swear 罵髒話

7. He is giving me the silent treatment.　他在跟我冷戰。

silent 寂靜的／treatment 對待

「若無其事原來是最狠的報復！」的確，比起大吵大鬧、摔鍋摔盤，冷戰對於很多人來說反而更加難以承受！除了心理控管能力要強之外，還得做好持久戰的準備，超級消耗元氣的！當你遇到對方和你冷戰時，該怎麼和朋友訴苦呢？一起來看看！

• 關於「冷戰」，你還能這樣說：

I tried to talk to her but I was given the cold shoulder.
我試圖跟她溝通，但她拒絕溝通。

Molly won't even look at me.
Molly 正眼都不願意看我了。

She's been sulking all day.
她整天都在生悶氣。

give someone the cold shoulder 冷漠以待	sulk 生悶氣

8. I'm still holding a grudge.　我還在記仇。

hold a grudge 記仇

不管冷戰、熱戰，凡是吵架多少都會造成一定程度的心理疙瘩。很多時候，雖說時間會沖淡一切，但並不能使傷痕消失。如果你是那種吵架之後很難平復、調節過來的人，該怎麼表達你的心情呢？你可以這樣說……

• 關於「記仇」，你還能這樣說：

I'm not over it yet.
我還沒釋懷。

She's a vindictive woman.
她是個會記仇的女人。

Why not let bygones be bygones?

為什麼不能既往不咎呢？

over 放下	vindictive 記仇的	let bygones be bygones 既往不咎

9. Are you still mad at me?　你還在生我的氣嗎？

mad 生氣的

吵架之後，最令人難受的就是尷尬期了，當兩人都處於低氣壓中時，總要有一方先釋出善意，伸出 olive branch「橄欖枝」，現在我們就來學幾句非常好用的破冰句子吧！

• 關於「和好」，你還能這樣說：

I'm a pig. It's all my fault. Let's get over it?

我是豬，都是我的錯，我們和好吧？

It was wrong of me to have said that. Can you forgive me?

我那樣說話不對，你可以原諒我嗎？

What can I do to make up with him?

我要怎麼做才能跟他和好？

fault 錯誤	get over 從……恢復過來	forgive 原諒
make up 和好		

10. I think we should take a beat and get some coffee.

我覺得我們應該先緩緩，喝杯咖啡。

> take a beat 暫緩

加強軍備的目的不是為了發動戰爭，而是避免戰爭。同樣地，學完了如何應對吵架，我們也應該來學學如何善用溝通技巧避免紛爭。希望這些句子用起來，真的能幫助到你在面臨即將發生的衝突時，能夠以和代戰，同時順利完成溝通喔！

• 關於「化解衝突」，你還能這樣說：

Let's not get personal here.
我們不要人身攻擊。

I agree with what you said, but please try to understand my point of view.
我同意你說的，但請你試著理解一下我的想法。

I know we had our bumps, but I think we need to sit down and talk things through.
我知道我們有過不開心，但我覺得我們應該坐下來好好談談。

personal 個人的	agree 同意	point of view 觀點
bump 顛簸	talk things through 講清楚	

 跟吵架有關的慣用語

1. punching bag 出氣包

哈哈：He just started shouting at me for no reason!
他就開始對我大吼大叫。

Lyla：I feel for you, but you really make a good punching bag sometimes!
我非常同情你，但你有時候真的滿適合當出氣包的！

2. agree to disagree　求同存異

哈哈：Since we can never reach a consensus on that, let's agree to disagree.

因為我們無法達成共識，那我們倒不如求同存異，各持己見吧！

Lyla：I disagree!

我不同意！

3. It takes two to make a quarrel.　一個巴掌拍不響

哈哈：She is the one in the wrong!

這次是她的錯！

Lyla：It takes two to make a quarrel. You should check yourself too.

一個巴掌拍不響的，你也要檢討一下自己。

4. fight like cat and dog　爭吵不休

哈哈：Should I invite Yvette as well?

我該不該邀 Yvette 呢？

Lyla：Never! You can't put Yvette and Celine together. They always fight like cat and dog.

千萬不要！你不能把 Yvette 和 Celine 放在一起，他們一定會吵翻天！

5. add fuel to the fire　火上澆油

哈哈：She's being difficult. I think I should call her and have it out with her.

她又在搞事了，我覺得我要打給她跟她講清楚。

Lyla：No! Don't add fuel to the fire. Just leave her alone.

不要！別再火上澆油了，你就別理她吧！

第 21 章　哈啦朋友

角色：哈哈（來自台灣）、Lyla（來自美國）

有人説在國外求學時很難交到當地真正的好朋友，除了因為文化差異和語言隔閡外，更關鍵的往往是自己不敢突破舒適圈，只願意和説相同語言的人待在一起。但其實有時候，只要具備幾句常用的 icebreaker「破冰話題」，和真誠的心（而不是只企圖想練英語），對方是願意包容我們笨拙的語言，進而深交的。現在，我們就一起來聊聊關於「朋友」的各種英文會話吧！

1. I usually hang out with James.　我通常會跟 James 一起出去玩。

> hang out　出去玩

「和……一起玩」最簡單、最常見的英文表達就是 hang out with 或 hang around with。特別注意，如果是 go out with 通常有「和……約會」的意思喔！因此，如果要説：「我和 James 是朋友。」我們可以説 I hang out with James.。

• 關於「和……是朋友」，你還能這樣説：

Susan is my best friend here.
Susan 是我這裡最好的朋友。

She's a good friend of mine.
她是我的好朋友。

Dustin and I are great buddies.
我和 Dustin 是好朋友。

> **buddy** 好朋友

2. Harry, this is Merlin. Merlin, this is Harry.

Harry，這位是 Merlin。Merlin，這位是 Harry。

> this 這位

雖然非常老梗，但非常好用！介紹兩個朋友互相認識時，就說這句：This is...This is...「這位是……，這位是……。」這時，兩位朋友便會開始互相：Hi!、Nice to meet you!

• 關於「介紹朋友認識」，你還能這樣說：

Let me introduce you to Heinrich. He's my favorite colleague.
讓我介紹一下 Heinrich，他是我最愛的同事。

Have you met Lucy? She is my flat mate.
你見過 Lucy 了嗎？她是我室友。

I'd like you to meet Duke. He's also a huge Beatles fan.
我想讓你見見 Duke，他也是一位披頭四的忠實粉絲。

introduce 介紹	colleague 同事	flat mate 室友
huge 大的		

3. Jenny and I have a lot in common.　我和 Jenny 有很多共通點。

> have...in common 有……共通點

介紹自己的朋友時，我們可先回溯一下和他／她認識的過程。如果一開始是因為趣味相投，彼此有許多共通點，我們可以說：...and I have a lot in common.「……和我有許多共通點。」或 We hit it off.「我們一拍即合。」如果一開始並不太喜歡對方，我們可以說：I didn't like him at first.「我一開始不喜歡他。」、I started out not liking her, but later she broke the image she had in my head.「我一開始不喜歡她，但後來她打破了我對她的印象。」、I thought he was quite stuck-up when I first met him.「我第一次見他時以為他是個很驕傲的人。」

- 關於「如何認識的」，你還能這樣說：

We hit it off straight away.
我們一拍即合。

We went to the same primary school and we've been close friends since.
我們上同一所小學，從那時我們就一直很好。

I know him through a friend.
我跟他是透過朋友認識的。

hit if off 一拍即合	straight away 立刻	primary school 小學
since 自從當時	through 透過	

4. It's been so long! 好久不見了！

long 久

遇到許久不見的老友，每個人都會說一句「好久不見！」。除了 Long time no see! 之外，我們也來學學更多道地的表達法。如：It's been so long!「好久不見了！」這句的完整意思是：It's been so long since I last saw you.「距離上次見到你已經過了好久了。」但日常的對話中，通常只會說簡短版的。

- 關於「好久不見」，你還能這樣說：

Long time no see! How have you been?
好久不見！最近還好嗎？

I haven't seen you for ages. I didn't recognize you.
我好久沒見到你了，我幾乎認不出你了。

It's been quite a while.
好久不見了。

long time no see 好久不見	ages 很長一段時間	recognize 辨認
quite 相當	a while 一段時間	

5. He's helped me through the toughest times. He means a lot to me.　他幫我度過最艱難的時期，他對我來說非常重要。

> tough　艱難的／ time　時期／ mean　意義

人生中能交到一個生死之交等級的朋友，著實不枉此生了。因此，我們應當來學學怎麼跟別人介紹這些生命中的摯友。最常見的兩句便是：He means a lot to me.「他對我來說非常重要。」和 He's my brother.「他是我兄弟。」女生之間則是用 bestie「閨蜜」這個字，如：She's my bestie.「她是我閨蜜。」外，要表達「可傾訴的對象」則可以說：She's always a shoulder to cry on for me.「她對我來說一直是一個精神依靠。」

• 關於「真摯的友情」，你還能這樣說：

He's not just another fair-weather friend. He's the one I can fully trust.
他不只是一個酒肉朋友，而是我可以真正相信的人。

You and Ian seem pretty tight.
你和 Ian 感情好像很好。

He's like a brother to me. I know he is always there for me when I need him.
他和我情同手足。我知道當我需要他的時候，他一定都在。

fully　完全	trust　信任	seem　似乎
tight　感情好	fair-weather friend　酒肉朋友	

6. My lips are sealed.　我誰都不會說。

> lips　嘴唇／ seal　密封

朋友之間交換祕密是一種對彼此信任的象徵，因此，當對方向自己透露祕密時，我們可以用以下句子來回應，表示自己是可靠的、可信任的。

- 關於「信任朋友」，你還能這樣說：

It is just between us.
這件事我只告訴你。

I won't tell a soul.
我不會跟任何人講。

I know I can always count on you.
我就知道我一定可以信任你。

between 在……之間	**soul** 靈魂	**count on** 信賴

7. We don't really get along. 　我們處得不太好。

get along 相處得好

get along 或 get along well 意思是「處得很好」，而如果要表達「處不來」，我們可以說：We don't really get along.「我們處得不太好。」或 I can't stand her.「我受不了她了。」、I'm tired of her constant whining.「我受夠了她一直在抱怨。」

- 關於「關係不好」，你還能這樣說：

I am not on speaking terms with Vivian.
我不跟 Vivian 來往了。

We don't talk anymore.
我們沒有來往了。

From now on, he's dead to me.
從現在起，他對我來說已經死了。

not on speaking terms with 不與……來往	**dead** 死掉的

8. You ratted me out!　你出賣我！

rat out　告發

「出賣」我們可以用直譯的 sell 這個字，如：He sold me out.「他出賣我。」或 He ratted me out.「他出賣我。」同義詞還有 betray 和 backstab。其中，backstab 直譯的意思就是「背後捅刀」，相當傳神吧！

- 關於「背叛朋友」，你還能這樣說：

How could you? I trusted you!
你怎麼可以這樣？我之前相信你的！

He's a total backstabber. Stay away from him.
他是個會暗算別人的小人。請遠離他。

You betrayed me!
你背叛我。

trust　信任	backstabber　暗算他人的人	betray　背叛

9. I got your back.　我罩你。

got one's back　支持某人

比起亞洲人，西方人通常有更多的 PDA（public display of affection）「於公眾場合展現情感」。因此，和「老外」打交道時，我們通常可以感受到對方的熱情，原因之一便是他們常掛在嘴邊的以下幾句話。

- 關於「朋友間常說的話」，你還能這樣說：

You got it! Bro!
沒問題！

Anytime bud!
別客氣！

You're my man.
你是我的好兄弟！

> **bud** 好朋友

10. I'm not a people person.　我不太擅長社交。

> people person 善於社交的人

people person 這個詞乍看之下很奇怪，怎麼會同時出現複數型的 people 和單數型的 person 呢？其實，它就是指「善於社交的人」或「喜歡人群的人」。因此，如果要說自己是個「邊緣人」，我們可以說：I'm not a people person.「我不太擅長社交。」另外，misfit 和 loner 兩個名詞都可以表示「邊緣人」。如：I'm a loner. I'm always on my own.「我是個邊邊，老是自己一個人。」

- 關於「邊緣人」，你還能這樣說：

I don't enjoy socializing and being with people.
我不喜歡社交，和人群在一起。

I just don't seem to be able to fit in at the new school.
我在這所新的學校好像就是無法融入。

Although being surrounded by people, I still feel so left out deep down.
雖然被人群包圍著，我內心深處還是覺得被遺棄。

socialize 社交	fit in 融入	surround 圍繞
left out 被遺棄的	deep down 內心深處	

跟朋友有關的慣用語

1. strike up a friendship with   和……做朋友

哈哈：Peter is actually pretty funny! I'd like to strike up a friendship with him.

Peter 其實很好玩欸！我想要和他做朋友。

Lyla：You don't want to be his friend. He's a total jerk.

千萬不要！他是個混蛋。

2. through thick and thin   福禍與共

哈哈：So you've known Abby for 15 years! That's a long time!

妳和 Abby 認識十五年了啊！好久喔！

Lyla：Yeah! We've been together through thick and thin.

對啊！我們一起經歷過好多事。

3. two peas in a pod   個性相像

哈哈：You guys are like two peas in a pod.

你們兩個個性也太像了吧！

Lyla：I get this a lot. People always say we're like twins.

大家都這麼說。還說我們像雙胞胎一樣。

4. on the same wavelength   合得來

哈哈：We're usually on the same wavelength, but this time I really can't agree with her.

我們通常挺合得來的，但這次我真的無法同意她。

Lyla：I'm with you on this. She's a bit drastic this time.

我站你這邊，她這次有點極端了。

5. clear the air   化解紛爭

哈哈：I think you need to clear the air with Jessica first.

我覺得妳要先和 Jessica 解決一下你們的爭執吧！

Lyla：No way! I will never talk to her again.

不可能！我再也不會和她講話了。

第 22 章 哈啦父母

角色：哈哈（來自台灣）、Lyla（來自美國）

講到父母，大家的第一想法是什麼呢？管東管西？嘮叨煩人？還是知心好友？無話不談？我們在人生的每個階段，隨著自己和父母的距離忽遠忽近，對於父母的情感都會有微妙的轉變。而東西方文化對於父母角色的理解也有所差異，造成了當我們和外國人聊父母時，時常會感受到不小的文化衝擊。本章節整理了十種最常聊到的「爸媽經」，一起來讀讀吧！

1. My father is a bank manager. 我爸爸是一位銀行經理。

> manager 經理

一開始我們先來說說如何介紹父母的職業、家中排行及來自哪裡。在英文中，問別人的職業一般不會用 What is your father's job?，而是 What does your father do?「你爸爸是做什麼的？」而回答時可以直接說：My father is a...「我爸爸是一位……。」介紹到父母的家庭時，我們可以說：My mother is one of... children.「我媽有……個兄弟姊妹。」如果是獨生子女，則是 the only child。最後，介紹父母來自哪裡時，如果要明確表示「祖籍」，我們可以加上 originally「原本」這個字，比如說：My mother is originally from Jamaica.「我媽媽的祖籍在雅買加。」

• 關於「介紹父母」，你還能這樣說：

My mom is one of five children.
我媽有四個兄弟姊妹。

My parents live in Canada, so I don't see them often.
我父母住在加拿大，所以我不常和他們見面。

My grandparents on my mother's side are originally from Mexico.
我外公、外婆原本是來自墨西哥的。

originally 原本	Mexico 墨西哥

2. My mother is strict with me, but also gives me a lot of freedom.　我媽對我很嚴格，但也給我很多自由。

strict 嚴格的／freedom 自由

關於父母的管教方式，這邊介紹兩個片語：helicopter parent「直升機家長」和 micromanager「控制狂」。如果父母過度干預孩子的生活，就像直升機一般地盤旋在四周，叨叨不休，這時候他們就是所謂的 helicopter parents 了。另外一個近義詞 micromanager 意思也差不多。這個詞的詞首 micro 意思是「細微」，manager 表示「掌管者」。因此，micromanager 就是用來指稱那些連衣服穿什麼、三餐吃什麼都要插手干預的控制狂父母。

- 關於「父母管教」，你還能這樣說：

My parents don't seem to care about me.
我爸媽好像都不管我。

My father is a helicopter parent.
我爸是位直升機家長。

I have a micromanaging father.
我有一個管東管西的爸爸。

seem 似乎	helicopter parent 直升機家長	micromanaging 東管西的

3. My mom is a worry-wart.　我媽很會操心。

worry-wart 很會擔心的人

父母操心子女這很正常，但如果你的父母是有凡事會日夜操煩的 tendency「趨向」，那可能就會造成一點點的壓迫感了。這種子女的各種大小事都時常糾結於心的人，我們可以稱為 worry-wart，也就是「很會擔心的人」。比如，我們可以說：My mom is a worry-wart. She gets paranoid about me all the time.「我媽很會操心，她老是因為我感到焦慮。」

- 關於「父母操心子女」，你還能這樣說：

My mother worries too much about me.
我媽太擔心我了。

My father is the most fearful, nervous, anxious person I've ever known.
我爸是我見過最容易緊張、最容易擔心東擔心西的人了。

My mother has a tendency to worry too much about me.
我媽媽容易太過擔心我。

worry 擔心	fearful 害怕的	anxious 焦慮的
tendency 趨向		

4. It's exhausting to be around my father. 跟我爸相處實在太累了。

exhausting 令人精疲力竭的

人們總是折磨自己最親近的人。因此，家人之間產生的矛盾和衝突往往是最多的。想當然，從小到大和自己朝夕相處的爸媽，一定也有很多吐槽點。這些在英文中要怎麼說呢？

- 關於「和父母關係不好」，你還能這樣說：

There's a lot of tension between me and my mother.
我和我媽媽的關心挺緊張的。

We weren't speaking for three years in a row.
我們連續三年都沒有講過話。

My relationship with my mom was a bit rocky before.
我和我媽媽的關係以前有點惡劣。

tension 緊張	in a row 連續	relationship 關係
rocky 不穩定的		

5. Respect your father.　對爸爸要尊敬。

> respect 尊敬

西方社會沒有完全對應的「孝順」概念。即使是 filial piety「孝順」，蘊含的也是從華人文化遷移過去的概念，而不是原本就存在於歐美文化中的。在表達類似「孝順」的意思時，他們通常是用 love 或 respect 來表達。圍繞著這個概念，讓我們一起來看看英語口語中還有哪些方式可以表達中文的「孝順」的意思。

- 關於「孝順父母」，你還能這樣說：

I need to be a better son.
我還不夠孝順。

She is not a good daughter.
她不是很孝順。

Listen to your dad!
聽你爸爸的話！

son 兒子	daughter 女兒

6. My dad means the world to me.　我爸爸就是我的整個世界。

> mean the world to... 對……來說很重要

西方人表達愛通常是直球投射，情感滿溢的。來看看這幾個「表達對父母的愛」的英文句子，你能不能感受到和天一樣寬、跟海一樣深的極致表現呢？

- 關於「表達對父母的愛」，你還能這樣說：

I have the best dad in the world.
我有一個世界上最好的爸爸。

Dad, you are a hero.
老爸，你是我的英雄。

Wherever I am, I know my mom is always there.
無論我在哪，我知道我媽媽一直都會在我身旁。

wherever 無論在哪

7. Mick is a mama's boy.　Mick 是一個媽寶。

mama's boy　媽寶

「媽寶」還真有一個對應的英文片語叫 mama's boy。當然，形容女生的話就是 daddy's girl 囉！有時候，和那些媽寶男、媽寶女打交道時是不是感到相當無言，忍不住想吐槽一番呢？

• 關於「靠爸靠媽族」，你還能這樣說：

She is such a daddy's girl.
她真是個靠爸族啊！

Don't be a spoiled brat.
別再當個被寵壞的孩子。

He's too emotionally attached to his mother.
他心理上太依賴他媽媽了。

spoil　寵壞	brat　小孩子	emotionally　情緒上
attach　依附		

8. My family is very close.　我們家人之間非常親近。

close　親近的

有人說，父母與孩子之間的關係再緊密也比不過父母之間的關係深厚。可以說父母的關係融洽，幾乎就等於一個快樂的家庭。如果你幸運地生在一個關係和睦的家庭，你可以說：My family is very close.「我們家人之間非常親近。」相反的，父母關係不好，則可以說：My parents aren't getting on too well together.「我父母相處地不是很好。」

• 關於「父母之間關係」，你還能這樣說：

I have the good fortune of having a happy, close-knit family.
我很幸運能有一個和樂且緊密的家庭。

There was a lot of fighting at home.
那時候家裡常常吵假。

My parents aren't getting on too well together.

我父母相處地不是很好。

fortune 運氣	close-knit 緊密的	fighting 吵架
get on well 相處地融洽		

9. My parents got divorced when I was in college.

我父母在我大學的時候離婚了。

divorce 離婚

「離婚」一般會用 divorce 這個詞，口語上也有時候會説 break up 或 split up。be divorced 表示「離婚的狀態」，而 get divorced 則是「離婚本身這個動作」。另外，和離婚相關的幾個表達有：My dad had custody of me.「我爸擁有我的撫養權。」、I stayed with my father.「我跟我爸爸。」、I visit my father once a month.「我一個月去找我爸一次。」等。至於，「繼父」、「繼母」的英文則是 stepfather 和 stepmother，如：Sam is not my father by blood. He's my stepfather.「Sam 不是我的親生父親，他是我繼父。」

• 關於「父母離異」，你還能這樣說：

I grew up in a single-parent family.

我在一個單親家庭長大。

They've been divorced for ten years.

他們已經離婚十年了。

We're separated.

我們分居了。

single-parent family 單親家庭	divorce 離婚	separate 分居

10. Be careful!　小心！

careful 小心的

天下父母心，不管在哪裡，父母時時叮嚀的話語聲，聽起來似乎都大同小異。你在看電視的時候：「該寫作業啦！」你在切菜的時候：「小心喔！」你在吵著要買東西的時候：「再說吧！」這些情境是不是很寫實、很熟悉呢？讓我們一起來看看這些父母甜蜜的嘮叨聲用英語怎麼說！

• 關於「父母常說的話」，你還能這樣說：

Do your homework.
做你的作業。

What did I just say?
我剛剛說什麼？

We'll see.
再說吧！

homework 作業

 跟父母有關的慣用語

1. spitting image　長得極為相像

哈哈：Did you see Rachel and her mother? They look so much alike.
　　　妳有看到 Rachel 和她媽媽嗎？她們長得好像啊！

Lyla：Yes. I was gonna say she's the spitting image of her mom.
　　　對啊！我才想說她和她媽媽簡直是同一個模子印出來的。

2. The apple doesn't fall far from the tree.　有其父必有其子（女）。

哈哈：Brian's son is showing his own athletic talent.
　　　Brian 的兒子開始展現出他自己的運動天賦了。

Lyla：The apple doesn't fall far from the tree.
有其父必有其子。

3. father figure　如父親般的存在

Lyla：I'm gonna miss him so much. He's been a father figure to me.
我一定會很想他的。他對我來說就像一個父親一樣。

哈哈：Yeah! Yeah! Yeah! Just admit you like her.
好好好！妳就承認妳喜歡他吧！

4. not your father's...　可是很先進的……

哈哈：Are you sure about this? A five-thousand-dollar laptop?
妳確定嗎？這台筆電要五千美元欸！

Lyla：Come on! It's not your father's laptop. Everything is state-of-the-art!
拜託！這可不是什麼上個世紀的破電腦欸！它所有配件都是最先進的！

5. a chip off the old block　和老爸或老媽一個樣

哈哈：I'm going to the university my father went to.
我要去讀我爸讀過的大學。

Lyla：You're a chip off the old block.
你怎麼什麼都跟你老爸一樣。

第 23 章　哈啦家鄉

角色：哈哈（來自台灣）、Lyla（來自美國）

家鄉是自己的身份，也是在外遇到挫折時最想躲回去的一個地方，不管它再破再舊，它都是我們的家。學會介紹自己的家鄉是很重要的。在各種社交場合，或很多語言考試中，都需要我們介紹自己的家鄉。家鄉也是我們初識彼此時最常聊到的話題之一。現在，就讓我們一起來學學如何用英文介紹自己的家鄉。

1. I was born and raised in Melbourne, Australia.

我在澳洲墨爾本出生長大。

born 出生／ raise 撫養長大／ Melbourne 墨爾本／ Australia 澳洲

回答 Where are you from?「你是哪裡人？」有很多種方式，其中，一個在口語中常聽到又不失正式的說法是：I was born and raised in...「我在……出生長大。」記住，講英文時要先從小地方講到大地方，比如要說「我在美國紐約出生長大。」時，我們會說：I was born and raised in New York, America.

• 關於「我的家鄉」，你還能這樣說：

I'm from New York.
我來自紐約。

I live in Taipei, but I'm originally from Paris.
我住在台北，但我原本是來自巴黎。

I come from Luxembourg, a small country in Europe.
我來自盧森堡，一個歐洲的小國家。

Luxembourg 盧森堡	Europe 歐洲

2. It is a big international city. 它是一個大的國際化的城市。

> international 國際化的

當別人問：What's your hometown like?「你的家鄉是一個怎樣的地方呢？」時，怎麼回答呢？我們可以說：It's a big city.「它是一座大城市。」、It's a small town.「它是一座小城鎮。」、It's a small village.「它是一座小村莊。」、It's a beach place.「它是一個海邊城市。」等。

• 關於「描述家鄉」，你還能這樣說：

It's a very nice, medium-sized city.
它是一座很棒的中型城市。

It's in a very beautiful part of England.
它在英格蘭很美的一個區域。

We do have some high buildings, but there's not a lot.
我們是有幾座比較高的建築，但不多。

medium-sized 中型的	building 建築物

3. It's famous for its nature. 它以自然景觀聞名。

> famous 有名的／ nature 自然景觀

描述家鄉特色時，我們可以使用兩個常見的句型：be famous for「以……聞名」和 be famous as「以……身份而得名」，如：Taipei is famous for its street foods.「台北以它小吃聞名。」、Manchester is famous as an industrial city.「曼徹斯特是一座知名的工業城市。」另外，也可以用 It has... 和 There is...「它有」的句型。

• 關於「家鄉特色」，你還能這樣說：

San Francisco is best known for its amazing burgers.
舊金山最出名的就是它超美味的漢堡。

It has a lot of night markets.

它有很多夜市。

There are a lot of beautiful beaches.

那裡有很多美麗的海灘。

| San Francisco 舊金山 | known 為人所知的 | burger 漢堡 |
| night market 夜市 | beach 海灘 | |

4. There's a lot of attractions.　那裡有很多旅遊景點。

attraction 景點

我們都知道：There is ＋單數名詞；There are ＋複數名詞。但在口語會話中，無論名詞單複數，大家常常把 There's 當作一個固定的句子開頭，因此，我們常常也會聽到像 There's a lot of attractions.「那裡有很多旅遊景點。」這種句子。而同樣的意思，我們也可以用地名來開頭，如：Tainan has a lot of history.「台南有很豐富的歷史文化。」

• 關於「家鄉活動」，你還能這樣說：

There's a lot more to do than you see in those guidebooks.

你能去玩的地方比那些旅遊書上寫得多太多了。

Someone says Budapest is all about drinking and partying.

有人説去布達佩斯就是要喝酒、開趴。

If you've never been on a pub crawl, you can't say you've been to England.

如果你沒參加過喝通關，就不要説你去過英格蘭。

| guidebook 旅遊指南 | Budapest 布達佩斯 | party 開派對 |
| pub crawl 跑酒吧喝通關 | | |

5. It's quite a busy city. Very crowded. Crazy traffic.
那裡生活很繁忙、很擁擠，塞車超嚴重。

> crowded 擁擠的／ traffic 交通擁堵

你的家鄉生活是什麼樣子的呢？是車水馬龍、熙攘喧囂，還是好山好水、悠閒愜意？在英文中，這些表達其實比你想像的更簡單喔！

- 關於「家鄉生活」，你還能這樣說：

It's easy going. People come there to retire.
那裡非常放鬆，很多退休人士會去那裡。

It's a pleasant place to live.
那裡很適合居住。

It was rated one of the best cities to live in America.
它被選為美國最適合居住的城市。

easy going 令人放鬆的	retire 退休	pleasant 令人愉快的
rate 評選		

6. People from Sydney might come across as a little rude.
雪梨人可能給人的印象是比較沒禮貌。

> Sydney 雪梨／ come across as 似乎／ rude 無禮的

很常有人說：一個地方最美的風景是人，但旅遊經驗豐富的人也常說到某某地方的人給旅客帶來不小的驚魂。你家鄉的人是怎麼樣的呢？一起來學學幾個好用又不流於俗套的句子吧！

- 關於「家鄉的人」，你還能這樣說：

People there are very friendly to foreigners who'd come in.
那裡的人對外來遊客都很友善。

There are lots of nasty people.
那裡有很多惡質的人。

Usually originals from London are not very friendly.
通常倫敦本地人都不是太友善。

foreigner 外來人士	nasty 惡質的	original 本地人

7. My city has been growing a lot recently.　我住的城市最近發展得很快。

grow 成長／recently 最近

城市發展的速度令人瞠目結舌，也讓人不勝唏噓。綠地和樹林被建築和工廠逼得節節敗退，傳統店家抵擋不住連鎖企業的強勢擴張而倒閉，經常讓那些三五個月回一次家的返鄉人大嘆：「時代的眼淚啊！」而關於「城市擴張」，在英文中，我們可以説：It has expanded a lot.「它的規模成長了好多。」、It's been growing a lot.「它發展地好快。」相反地，一個地方如果維持老樣子，我們可以説：It hasn't changed that much at all.「它沒什麼太大的改變。」

The forest has been smaller than it used to be.
這座森林比起以前縮水很多了。

It's slightly more industrial than it once was.
這裡稍微比以前更工業化了。

Bangkok is almost unrecognizable compared to twenty years ago.
曼谷比起二十年前幾乎快認不出來了。

forest 森林	used to 曾經	slightly 稍微
industrial 工業化的	once 曾經	Bangkok 曼谷
unrecognizable 無法辨認的		compared to 比起

第23章 哈啦家鄉

217

8. It's home to one of the best universities in the country.
它有全國頂尖的大學。

> be home to 是……的歸屬／ university 大學／ country 國家

關於家鄉的教育、交通、物價和休閒活動，在英文中該怎麼介紹呢？我們可以用上一個句型：It's home to...「它有……。」比如：It's home to the largest city park in the country.「它有全國最大的城市公園。」、London is home to more than 800 cinemas.「倫敦有超過八百間電影院。」

- 關於「其他方面」，你還能這樣說：

There's a lot of good public transport.
那裡的公共交通運輸很不錯。

The cost of living is really high.
物價非常高。

There's not much for young people to do.
那裡沒什麼年輕人可以做的活動。

public transport 公共交通	cost of living 物價

9. Los Angeles is a mess.　洛杉磯超亂的。

> Los Angeles 洛杉磯

就像自家小孩一樣，人們吐槽家鄉時往往會鞭得格外大力，但當別人說到自己的城市或國家有任何不好時，那種「子不嫌母醜」的情緒就出現了。那不如……在被別人吐槽之前，自己先把它給吐個夠吧！

- 關於「吐槽家鄉」，你還能這樣說：

It's in the middle of nowhere.
它在一個鳥不生蛋的地方。

It struck me as a complicated soulless place.
它給我的感覺是一個很複雜而且沒什麼靈魂的地方。

Driving in the city can be a nightmare.
在這座城市裡開車跟做噩夢一樣。

in the middle of nowhere 鳥不生蛋的地方		strike 打擊
complicated 複雜的	soulless 沒有靈魂的	nightmare 惡夢

10. You appreciate your hometown once you're away from it.
你遠離家鄉時才能真正欣賞家鄉。

appreciate 欣賞／ hometown 家鄉／ once 一旦／ away 遠離

多少異鄉遊子因為現實因素背井離鄉，久久才能回一次家，又或長期回不了家，甚至已把陌生住成了熟悉。即便如此，家的熟悉卻永遠不會褪成陌生，只會永遠堅守、永遠等待歸來的你。遠離家鄉的你，思鄉的話，去跟身邊的朋友聊聊你的家鄉吧！

- 關於「遠離家鄉」，你還能這樣說：

I haven't been back for twenty years.
我已經二十年沒回去了。

I miss my home so much.
我好想家啊！

I'd always come back to visit my hometown even though I've moved to London.
即便我現在搬到倫敦了，我還是很常回我的家鄉。

hometown 家鄉	even though 即便

1. out of town 出城

哈哈：We're having a barbecue party on Saturday. You coming?
我們這星期六要辦一場烤肉趴，妳要來嗎？

Lyla：Sucks I'm gonna be out of town.
可惜我要去外地。

2. come to town 到來

哈哈：Christmas is coming to town! Anything planned?
聖誕節快到了！有什麼計畫嗎？

Lyla：I'm going back to America to meet up with my mom.
我要回美國和我媽見面。

3. paint the town red 外出狂歡

哈哈：Finally got our report done! What a load off!
終於把報告完成了！真是鬆了一口氣！

Lyla：We're gonna paint the town red tonight!
今晚我們要出去狂歡！

4. hometown honey 青梅竹馬

哈哈：Duke is getting married with his hometown honey.
Duke 要和他的青梅竹馬結婚了！

Lyla：Finally! They've been together for almost twelve years.
終於啊！他們已經交往快十二年了！

5. the land of milk and honey 富饒之地

哈哈：I so want to move to New Zealand!
我好想搬去紐西蘭阿！

Lyla：So do I. It's the land of milk and honey.
我也是啊！那裡真是個富饒之地。

第 24 章 哈啦回憶

角色：哈哈（來自台灣）、Lyla（來自美國）

Lyla 口中的 Throwback Thursday 就是在社群媒體上很流行的 #TBT，也就是每週四在 Facebook、Instagram 或 Twitter 上發佈各種懷舊的照片，並附註 #TBT，引起網友的討論，並藉此分享彼此的回憶。今天不管是不是星期四，都讓我們一起跌進回憶的漩渦，throwback to the good old days!

1. I was born in 1990, just one year before the Soviet Union collapsed. 我出生於 1990 年，也就是蘇聯解體的前一年。

born 出生的

你是幾年出生的呢？你出生的年代有什麼特殊的歷史事件呢？下次當你自我介紹時，與其只說 I was born in 1990.「我出生於 1990 年。」，試試在後面加上 just one year before the Soviet Union collapsed.「也就是蘇聯解體的前一年。」對方一定一輩子都忘不掉喔！

• 關於「出生」，你還能這樣說：

I was born into a rich family.
我出生在一個富裕家庭。

I was born to a single mother.
我出生時我媽媽單親。

I was born in Taichung and moved to Taipei before I turned one.
我在台中出生，然後一歲前搬到台北。

| be born into 出生在 | single mother 單親媽媽 | turn 變成 |

2. I had a lovely childhood. 我的童年很美好。

lovely 美好的／ childhood 童年

我們通常想要講「我的童年很……」時，都會直覺地用 My childhood was...，雖然沒有錯，但我們可以學學另外一種說法：I had a...childhood.。很多時候後者才是口語上更常使用的說法。

• 關於「童年」，你還能這樣說：

My childhood is certainly an unusual one.
我有一個特別的童年。

When I think of my childhood, poor is the first word that comes to my mind.
當我想到我的童年時，貧窮是我最先會想到的詞。

I consider my childhood…meh.
我的童年很……無趣。

certainly 肯定	unusual 特別的	think of 想到
poor 貧窮	consider 認為	meh 無趣的

3. The first couple of years of secondary school were rough at times. 我中學時期的前幾年過得有點艱難。

a couple of 幾個／ secondary school 中學／ rough 艱難的／ at times 有時

對於很多人來說，求學時期的回憶再苦都是會回甘的。的確，人生再也沒有一段時期是即使辛苦都那麼單純、即使危險都充滿保護網的吧！現在，讓時光倒轉，回到那個穿著制服、背著書包的自己吧！

• 關於「求學階段」，你還能這樣說：

I used to go to that school when I lived in Vancouver.
我以前住溫哥華時曾經在那裡上過學。

I was always a top student in class.
我在班上一直都是前幾名的。

For as long as I can remember, school was hard for me.
在我的記憶中，學校生活都是很痛苦的。

Vancouver 溫哥華	top 頂尖的	hard 困難的

4. I used to be a naughty little boy.　我以前曾經是個調皮的小男孩。

> used to 曾經／ naughty 調皮的

聊到回憶，就不得不學 used to 這個結構。used to 表示過去存在的習慣，通常是持續好一陣子的，如：I used to work in a factory.「我之前曾經在工廠上班。」、I used to live in Shanghai.「我曾在上海住過一陣子。」、I used to like playing basketball.「我以前曾經喜歡打籃球。」注意，別把 used to 和 be used to 搞混了，be used to 是指「習慣……」，如：I am used to the weather here.「我習慣這裡的天氣了。」、I am used to getting up early.「我習慣早起了。」

• 關於「小時候的性格」，你還能這樣說：

I was a lively over-joyful child in school.
我以前在學校是個活潑而且過度歡樂的小孩。

I grew up shy and afraid.
我從小到大都很害羞、膽怯。

I was an introverted kid growing up.
我小時候是個內向的小孩。

| lively 活潑的 | over-joyful 過度歡樂的 | grow up 長大 |
| afraid 膽怯的 | introverted 內向的 | |

5. Looking back, my father was truly the light of my life.
現在回想起來，我爸爸真的是我生命中的一盞明燈。

> truly 真的

looking back「回想起來」也是聊回憶時一個很好用的結構，常用在句子的開頭，如：Looking back, my mother was a saint.「現在回想起來，我媽媽真是一個聖人。」、Looking back, that was a decisive moment of my life.「現在回想起來，當時是我人生中一個決定性的時刻。」當你在 look back「回憶過往」的時候，是否發現很多當時沒發覺的美好呢？

• 關於「回憶父母」，你還能這樣說：

As a child, I was closer to my mother.
小時候我和媽媽比較親。

My father was always busy with his work and we didn't really talk much.
我爸以前一直在忙他的工作，所以我們不太常說話。

I remember being taken to the park every evening by my mother when I was a child.
我記得小時候每天晚上常被我媽帶去那座公園。

as 身為	close 親近的

6. It was a throwback to our college days.　它讓我們回到了大學時光。

throwback 回溯／college 大學

throwback「回溯」一般作為名詞，字面上的意思是「往回丟」，像是把自己扔回過去的時光一樣，一般搭配 to ＋時間點，如：This film is a throwback to the fifties.「這部電影是對五零年代的緬懷。」另外，還有一個詞是 nostalgic「懷舊的」，名詞是 nostalgia「懷舊情懷」，這個詞是指對過去時光的嚮往和懷念，如：She remained nostalgic about the days in Korea.「她非常懷念她在韓國的日子。」

• 關於「懷念過去」，你還能這樣說：

I always feel nostalgic for my high school years when I hear the song.
我聽到這首歌時都會想起我高中的時光。

It really brings me back to the good old days.
它能帶我回到過去的美好時光。

I don't spend that much time dwelling on the past.
我不會花太多時間在回憶過去。

nostalgic 懷舊的	good old days 過去的美好日子	dwell on 老是想著
past 過去		

7. I really miss our laughs and talks.　我非常想念我們的歡笑和談話。

> miss 想念／ laugh 歡笑／ talk 談話

人生中的美好回憶裡，身邊多半都有自己最愛的家人和朋友。即使後來相隔異地，一旦聊起過去，還是能立刻從中獲得滿滿的能量。下次，和朋友敘舊時，你可以說：I really miss our laughs and talks.「我非常想念我們的歡笑和談話。」

• 關於「美好的回憶」，你還能這樣說：

That was the best time of my life.
那是我一生中最美好的回憶。

My greatest memory is when I went on vacation with my family.
我最棒的回憶是和我的家人一起去旅行。

We had great time playing games together.
我們一起玩各種遊戲玩得很開心。

go on vacation 去度假	have a great time 玩得開心

8. I often cringe at some awkward memories.
我常常想到一些尷尬的回憶就會整個人縮起來。

> cringe 畏縮／ awkward 尷尬的

有時突然想起某個尷尬或可怕的回憶時，臉都會不由自主地皺起來，心頭也會瞬間咯噔一下，接著就陷入一種難堪而難以自拔的情緒，這種心理症狀在英文中叫 cringe attack「羞愧綜合症」。要克服 cringe attack，需要一個強大的心理素質，只要自己不覺得尷尬，尷尬的就是別人！

- 關於「痛苦的回憶」，你還能這樣說：

My teacher always put me down.
我的老師老是罵我。

I was bullied a lot at school.
我以前在學校常被霸凌。

I've spent so many years coping with that sad memory.
我已經花了好幾年消化那次悲傷的回憶。

put down 奚落	bully 霸凌	cope with 處理

9. I just have a vague memory of my high school.
我對於高中時期的記憶已經很模糊了。

vague 模糊的／memory 記憶

memory 同時有「回憶」和「記憶力」的意思。如果要說自己的「記憶力不好」，我們可以說 My memory is bad.「我的記憶力很差。」或 My memory is paralyzed.「我的記憶力癱瘓了。」要說「記不清某事」，我們可以說 I can barely remember…，如：I can barely remember anything about college.「我大學的事都記不得了。」

- 關於「模糊的回憶」，你還能這樣說：

I don't remember much of the first few years of elementary school.
我記不太清楚小學前幾年的事情了。

I've long forgotten what he looked like.
我早就忘記他長什麼樣子了。

My memory has failed me. I can't remember it.
我的記憶不管用了，我不記得它了。

elementary school 小學	forget 忘記	fail 辜負

10. If I recall correctly, she went to the same senior high school as you. 如果我沒記錯，她是跟你上同一所高中的。

> recall 回憶／correctly 正確地／senior high school 高中

最後，我們來聊聊回憶時經常會說到的「如果我沒記錯的話」在英文中有哪些說法。if I recall correctly、if my memory is correct、if my memory serves me right 都很常聽到。另外，還可以說 if I'm not mistaken。

- 關於「確認記憶」，你還能這樣說：

If my memory serves me right, his name was Barack.
如果我沒記錯的話，他的名字是 Barack。

If my memory is correct, it was a rainy day.
如果我沒記錯的話，那天是個雨天。

Memories are coming back! Can't believe I really did that.
我想起來了！真不敢相信我真的做了那種事。

serve 服務	correct 正確的	rainy 下雨的

 跟回憶有關的慣用語

1. ring a bell　有印象

哈哈：Do you remember Chris the janitor in Woodland Court?
　　　妳還記得 Woodland 宿舍的舍監 Chris 嗎？

Lyla：That does not ring a bell.
　　　沒印象欸！

2. slip my mind　忘記了

哈哈：Why are you still here? I thought you had an online seminar to attend.
　　　妳怎麼還在這？妳不是要參加一場線上研討會嗎？

Lyla：Oh boy! It totally slipped my mind.

喔！天啊！我完全忘記了！

3. photographic memory　　超強的記憶力

哈哈：Trust me! I have a photographic memory. It was man-made.

相信我！我的記憶力超強的，我就記得它是人造的！

Lyla：Whatever! Keep telling yourself that. I told you it was formed by nature.

隨便你！你愛怎麼說就怎麼說吧！我說過它是自然形成的了。

4. refresh one's memory　　提醒某人

哈哈：I don't feel like going to class. Let me just stay here.

我不想去上課，讓我待在這裡吧！

Lyla：Let me refresh your memory! You have skipped two classes. You don't want to flunk the finals.

容我提醒你一下，你已經翹了兩堂課了，你的期末考最好不要不及格。

5. a trip down memory lane　　回憶往昔

哈哈：A class union party is always a trip down memory lane for me and my friends when we talk about our crazy high school days.

同學會一直是我和我朋友們回憶過去的一個時刻，我們都會大聊我們高中時期的那些瘋狂事蹟。

Lyla：Oh! I miss my friends too.

噢！我也好想我朋友喔！

第 25 章　哈啦社會

角色：哈哈（來自台灣）、Lyla（來自美國）

每個時代都有人說這個社會喧囂而紛擾，每個時代也都會有人出來標榜這是個糟透了的時代，但真相或許是：每個時代都有它攪動人心的不安因子，導致沒有一個社會可以氣定神閒地活在當下，沉澱出美好。聽來言重，但本章節不是要教你如何成為社會觀察家，而是單純以一個平凡老百姓的角度來談談現代社會中的各種現象。

1. Everything is changing so fast that it's so hard to keep up.

世事瞬息萬變，我們難以追趕得上。

> keep up　趕上

有人曾開玩笑說：現代社會的步調連速食店都跟不上了！ McDonald's, not fast enough anymore.「麥當勞都不夠快了。」究竟是速食店真的變慢了，還是人們的生活節奏越踩越急了呢？閉上眼，深呼吸，拖個拍，問自己：What's the rush?「幹嘛這麼急呢？」

- 關於「社會步調」，你還能這樣說：

We should try to take a step back and slow down a bit.
我們應該退一步，慢下來。

We are too afraid to be left behind.
我們太害怕會落後其他人。

Fast food isn't fast enough anymore.
連速食的速度也跟不上了。

step　步伐	afraid　害怕的	leave behind　使落後
enough　足夠		

2. We live in a dog-eat-dog world.

我們活在一個不是你死就是我活的世界。

> dog-eat-dog 你死我活的

現代社會競爭激烈，人們你爭我搶的畫面，是不是真的很像 dog-eat-dog「狗咬狗」呢？還有一個很形象的片語是 throw someone under the bus，字面意思是「把某人扔到公車底下」，猜得到是什麼意思嗎？如：He threw me under the bus for his own promotion. 意思就是「他為了他自己的升遷而陷害我。」是不是很有畫面感呢？

We live in a society where getting ahead in life is everything.
我們處在一個凡事都要爭第一的社會。

Everybody is out to pull each other down.
每個人都在互扯後腿。

Hong Kong is a competitive society.
香港是一個非常競爭的社會。

get ahead 領先	pull down 扯後腿	competitive 競爭的

3. Like it or not, it is the society we live in.

不管你喜不喜歡，這就是我們所在的社會。

> like it or not 不管你喜不喜歡／ society 社會

like it or not 意思是「不管你喜不喜歡」，也就是由不得你選擇，不管怎樣你都必須接受的意思。原句是 whether you like it or not，在非正式的口語對話中則是直接說 like it or not，如：You are gonna face the facts, like it or not.「你得面對現實，不管你喜不喜歡。」

• 關於「風氣墮落」，你還能這樣說：

It's been all downhill since the nineties.
自從九零年代以來一切就一直走下坡。

Everything is falling apart.
一切都崩壞了。

Let's face it. People are less ethical today.
我們必須承認，現在的人道德感都比較薄弱。

downhill 下坡	fall apart 崩壞	face 面對
less 更不	ethical 道德的	

4. There are a lot of crazy things going on out there.
現在有很多亂七八糟的事情一直在發生。

go on 發生

要表達「社會很亂」，我們可以説 The society is a mess.，或用 crazy things 來表示「亂七八糟的事情」，如：There are lots of crazy things going on out there.「現在有很多亂七八糟的事情一直在發生。」其中，going on 的意思是「持續在發生」，而 out there 是一個常用的表達法，表示「在外面」或「在某個特定的地方」。

• 關於「複雜的社會」，你還能這樣說：

Many things I just can't wrap my head around.
很多事情我都搞不懂。

Why are they always overcomplicating things?
為什麼他們老是把問題複雜化？

We live in a complicated world.
我們生活在一個複雜的世界。

wrap one's head around 理解	overcomplicate 過度複雜化	complicated 複雜的

5. All they are interested in is power and money.

他們感興趣的只是權力和金錢。

> interested 感興趣的／power 權力

「貪財」在英文中可以用 money-crazed 或 money-hungry 來形容。而如果要形容某人很「物質」，我們則可以用 materialistic「物質主義的」這個形容詞。除了金錢之外，另一個令人腐化的東西就是 power「權力」了。人們追求權力，因為權力給他們 a sense of superiority「優越感」；另一種人追求的不是權力本身，而是 the benefits that come with it「隨附權力而來的利益」。而這種爭權奪力的行為就是我們常聽到的 power game「權力遊戲」。

• 關於「人性貪婪」，你還能這樣說：

Money has become the measure of everything.
金錢已經成為一切事物的衡量標準。

Everything is about money.
一切都跟錢有關。

Our whole society is built on worshiping wealth.
我們的整個社會是建築在崇尚財富之上。

measure 衡量標準	society 社會	worship 崇尚
wealth 財富		

6. The good have to suffer with the bad.　好人為壞人所累。

> the good 好人／suffer 受苦／the bad 壞人

雖然很多超級英雄的電影都告訴我們：邪不勝正、正義終將得到伸張，但現實世界中，惡勢力卻像一堵永遠打不倒的高牆，面對它，再浩然的英雄之氣都只能憋回肚子裡。身處於這種壞人當道的時局，我們只能無奈地說：The good has to suffer with the bad.「好人為壞人所累。」

- 關於「壞人當道」，你還能這樣說：

Stupid people screw up everything.
蠢人什麼事都辦不好。

Greed and envy are ruling the country.
貪婪和妒忌主宰著這個國家。

Why do bad people prosper and good people suffer?
為什麼壞人活千年，好人不長命？

screw up 搞砸	greed 貪婪	envy 妒忌
rule 統治	prosper 興旺	

7. There's nothing we can do about it.　我們無能為力。

> nothing　沒有什麼

雖然聽起來很頹喪，但多數人談論社會議題時總喜歡以「無能為力」結尾，不是他們消極，而是小蝦米確實沒有太多能耐啊！在英文中，我們可以用 There's nothing we can do about it.「我們無能為力。」或 There's not much we can do.「我們能力有限。」來表達這種情緒。

- 關於「無能為力」，你還能這樣說：

It is what it is.
就是這樣，還能怎麼辦！？

It's beyond my capacity.
我無能為力。

I'm helpless against it.
我無能為力。

beyond 超越	capacity 能力	helpless 無助的
against 對抗		

8. She's got a lot of street smarts.　她具備很多在社會上處事待人的能力。

> street smart　在社會上處事的能力

所謂 street smart 的意思是「在社會上處事的能力」，通常這種能力並不是在書本或學校裡能學得到的，而是經過在社會上歷練打滾後所獲得的經驗。與 street smart 相對的是 book smart，也就是很會讀書的那種聰明。想要在社會上吃得開，很多時候 book smart 還真的派不上用場呢！

• 關於「社會人」，你還能這樣說：

You are smooth.
你好圓滑。

You are so diplomatic!
你好圓融啊！

I'm not good at dealing with people.
我不擅長和人打交道。

smooth　圓滑的	diplomatic　圓融的	deal with　處理

9. It was a different time.　今非昔比。

> different　不同的

這句話可能要有點年紀的人才講得出來吧！當我們真的講出 It was a different time.「今非昔比。」時，我們可能在某種程度上已成為了那個我們以前嫌惡的倚老賣老、故步自封的「老人」了吧！

• 關於「時代不同」，你還能這樣說：

People weren't as promiscuous as they are now.
以前的人不像現在這麼隨便。

Things are different now.
現在情況不一樣了。

A lot has changed over the years.
這幾年來很多東西都改變了。

promiscuous 淫亂的

10. That's true, but… 是沒錯，但是……

true 正確的

最後，我們來學學討論議題時經常會用到的幾個句子，用起來讓你的話語聽上去更加合理、流暢！首先，「先同意後提出反駁論點」是話輪轉換中非常常見的一種技巧，比如：That's true, but... 和 Yeah, but...「是沒錯，但是……。」這種說法可以讓自己的應對顯得更加理性，也能更順暢地銜接到自己接下來的論點。而如果要打岔，我們則可以說 Sorry, but... 或 I'm sorry, but...「不好意思，……。」如：I'm sorry, but you did not provide any evidence to back up your claim.「不好意思，你並沒有為你的論點提出任何支持性的證據。」

- 關於「討論用語」，你還能這樣說：

May I say something?
我可以說一下嗎？

Please let me finish.
請讓我說完。

As I was saying, …
就像我剛剛說的……。

as 如同

1. fat cat   有錢有勢的人

哈哈：I haven't had a raise in six years and my workload is insane.

我六年來都沒有調薪，而且我的工作量還多到爆。

Lyla：Blame your fat cat boss.

要怪就怪你那肥貓老闆吧！

2. beautiful people   上流社會的時髦人物

哈哈：Did you go to the banquet?

你有去那場宴會嗎？

Lyla：Yeah! Met a lot of phony beautiful people.

有啊！見到了很多假惺惺的富豪名媛。

3. grassroots   草根民眾

哈哈：What he just said made no sense to me. He totally missed the point.

他剛剛說的完全沒有道理，他根本沒有講到重點啊！

Lyla：He should try to view the problems from a grassroots perspective.

他應該試著以草根民眾的角度來檢視這些問題。

4. social ladder   社會階梯

哈哈：When will I ever get to the top of the social ladder?

我什麼時候才能爬到社會階層的頂端呢？

Lyla：Well...to put it in perspective, you're probably at the foot of Mount Everest.

嗯……這麼說好了，你現在可能是在聖母峰的山腳處吧！

5. high society   上流社會

哈哈：Winnie keeps saying her ultimate dream is to marry a diplomat.

Winnie 一直說她的終極夢想是嫁給一位外交官。

Lyla：She takes it the only way to the high society.

她認為那是通往上流社會的唯一一條道路。

語研力 E056

哈啦英文 1000 句：

「圖像導引法」，帶你破冰、不尬聊，自信、舒適、流暢地用英語閒聊人生大小事

精準的導引學習脈絡，學習有系統、有邏輯，也更有效！

作　　者	徐培恩（Ryan）◎著
顧　　問	曾文旭
出版總監	陳逸祺、耿文國
主　　編	陳蕙芳
繪　　者	徐培恩（Ryan）
封面設計	李依靜
內文排版	李依靜
法律顧問	北辰著作權事務所

印　　製	世和印製企業有限公司
初　　版	2021年09月
出　　版	凱信企業集團─凱信企業管理顧問有限公司
電　　話	（02）2773-6566
傳　　真	（02）2778-1033
地　　址	106 台北市大安區忠孝東路四段218之4號12樓
信　　箱	kaihsinbooks@gmail.com

定　　價	新台幣349元／港幣116元
產品內容	1書

總 經 銷	采舍國際有限公司
地　　址	235 新北市中和區中山路二段366巷10號3樓
電　　話	（02）8245-8786
傳　　真	（02）8245-8718

本書如有缺頁、破損或倒裝，
請寄回開企更換。
106 台北市大安區忠孝東路四段218之4號12樓
編輯部收

國家圖書館出版品預行編目資料

哈啦英文1000句：「圖像導引法」，帶你破
冰、不尬聊，自信、舒適、流暢地用英語閒聊
人生大小事／徐培恩（Ryan）著. -- 初版. -- 臺
北市：凱信企業集團凱信企業管理顧問有限公
司, 2021.09
　　面；　公分
ISBN 978-986-06836-4-6(平裝)

1.英語 2.會話 3.詞彙 4.讀本

805.188　　　　　　　　　　　110012130